DOE RUN
I0716513

ADVANCED PRAISE

DOE RUN

by Sean Jacques

"Sean Jacques knows the heart of the Ozarks, and puts that knowledge on full display in this sweltering debut. *Doe Run* burns slow like good bourbon. Drink up."

—**Eli Cranor**, author of ***Don't Know Tough*** and ***Broiler***

"Recalling grit lit titans like Larry Brown and Daniel Woodrell, Jacques delivers the kind of Old Testament country noir that lives with you long after the last page. *Doe Run* is a beautifully rendered Ozark drama, a tale of friendship, grief and small-town tragedy by a storyteller who knows the land and his people down to the core. With prose that pops like birdshot and paints with stunning authenticity the hardscrabble hills of southwest Missouri, our 'hero' Pen Cullen may prove that You Can't Go Home Again but I will gladly return to the well if it's got Sean Jacques' name on it."

—**Peter Farris**, author of ***The Devil Himself***

"*Doe Run* is sitting smack in-between the poetic rumination of McCarthy and the Ozark mud of Woodrell. The novel delivers real pain and real evil but also a real shot at redemption, which is rare in this genre. But don't be mistaken, Sean Jacques still delivers a tale with teeth on par with any Peckinpah film. If you let yourself be immersed in the story, it will linger with you long after you finish."

—**Brian Panowich**, author of ***Nothing But the Bones***

"In this simmering debut, Sean Jacques renders the lives of his desperate characters with care and empathy, but doesn't hold back when it all boils over."

—**Scott Von Doviak**, author of ***Lowdown Road***

MORE PRAISE FOR
DOE RUN

"***Doe Run*** is an unflinching portrait of grief, lost love, and the long, haunting shadows of the past. This gritty tale lays bare the darkest depths of the human condition, and the flawed, rough-hewn characters will undoubtedly stick with you. With prose as spare and sharp as barbed wire, Sean Jacques delivers the goods with his impressive debut."

—**Scott Blackburn**, author of *It Dies with You*

"Like a cigarette butt tossed into the underbrush, ***Doe Run*** smolders. Haunted by their pasts, these characters are hunting for redemption, but are trapped in mires of betrayal and generational trauma. Fueled by fury and whiskey, they chase one bad idea after another in this rural noir tale of desperation where the coals burn bright under the leaf litter, just waiting to set the forest alight, as Jacques fans the flames with twists and secrets."

—**Meagan Lucas**, author of *Songbirds and Stray Dogs*

"In ***Doe Run***, Sean Jacques has assembled an entire slate of lonely characters yearning to find their way in a broken world, and he tells their stories with depth and compassion. This is a rural noir full of pathos and grit—and it absolutely deserves your attention."

—**C.W. Blackwell**, author of *Hard Mountain Clay*

DOE RUN

a novel

SEAN JACQUES

SHOTGUN HONEY

2 0 2 4

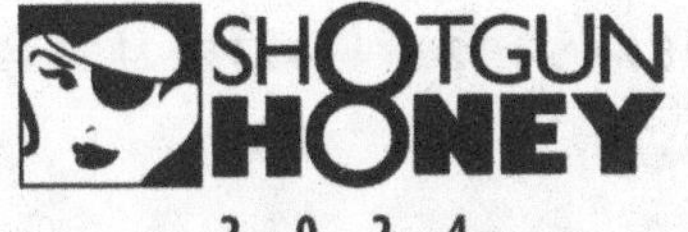

Published by **Shotgun Honey Books**

215 Loma Road
Charleston, WV 25314
www.ShotgunHoney.com

Cover by Bad Fido.

First Printing 2024.

ISBN-10: 1-956957-30-8
ISBN-13: 978-1-956957-30-3

9 8 7 6 5 4 3 2 1   24 23 22 21 20 19

To all the relations I shared an experience with
while growing up in Southern Missouri.
Your spirit has never left me, and never will.

DOE RUN

He's gone, no sign, no word of him; and I inherit
trouble and tears—and not for him alone,
the gods have laid such other burdens on me.
                    —Homer, *The Odyssey*

THREE DAYS UNTIL
DEER SEASON

1

THE DRIVER HAD BEEN BEHIND the wheel for twelve hours straight, save for the few pullovers to piss or refill the tank. Squatted low in the bucket seat, his back felt as if a middleweight had been kidney-punching him for twelve rounds, and with a dense morning fog veiling the glow of the new dawn, his blood-shot eyes were straining to follow the faint lines on the curvy highway.

Thirteen years, his mind kept counting. Thirteen years since he'd last driven over these Ozark hills. But with every blind bend he came to on the winding road, another ghost was waiting on the other side, and they were making him feel as if he'd never left for a day. Childhood recollections, mostly. Soft whispers from his dead mother. Beatings from his rotten father. Or some other bitter recollection of his roots, each one rising in the mist like a hellish phantom to remind him only death could have dragged him back here.

Thirteen years.

Figuring a hit of nicotine might ease his nagging aches, he reached inside the console for a Camel. He found the pack empty of hope. He crushed it then leaned to open the glovebox, and there sat a fresh pack on top of a Colt .45 and a box of bullets.

He grabbed the smokes and chewed off the cellophane and foil and lifted out the first lucky stick. His fingers dug into his shirt pocket and pulled out a silver Zippo. He flicked on the flame and as the Camel married the fire, his eyes came up to catch a blurred glimpse of some shape hurtling across the highway--he jerked the wheel and stomped the brake and the tires screamed. A violent thud came from the front end and the Firebird veered into a hard left and sailed down into a deep ravine until it hit dirt and came to a dead stop.

He sat there like a stone. The motor revving. His breaths short and rapid.

"Jesus Christ."

He shoved the gearshift into neutral. He checked himself in the rearview. His breaths coming in quick bursts. He looked behind to peer out the back window and saw gray sky.

"What the fuck?!"

He blew hard through his lips and reached for the door latch and bumped the door open. He leaned his head out and was greeted by a slap of cold November air. He pushed the door wide and stuck his boot out to the ground. He stretched his stiff back up from the bucket seat and hauled himself out of the car and was welcomed by a world of wintry trees and drifty vapors.

With razors running down his spine, he slow-shuffled toward the front of the Firebird. He found scratched paint and a shovelhead-size dent on the hood. Then saw the Nevada plate flopped down like a hand broken at the wrist.

"Shit."

He raised his eyes to the gray dawn, pestering it for an

explanation. With no answers coming, he became wondrous of the road-hurdling shape that had landed him in such misfortune.

Up the ravine he went, his anaconda boots slipping mightily on the dewy sage grass. When he perched the top, he caught sight of a yellow road sign with a black leaping buck.

It was plugged with six silver bullet holes.

He spat. Then he continued across the road, slowing his strides to cuss the skid marks burned by the Firebird's rubber, and upon reaching the other side, he spotted the white tail flashing in the high grass.

Down he dropped. He slow-stepped toward her. Then gaining within a few feet of where she was lying, her front legs went to jerking in the air. He squatted to ease her panic, appraising her broken body like a sawbone doctor might inspect a fading patient. Big brown marble eyes. A gray tongue draped out like an unformed fetus. Thick black-tan coat on her back and snow white from belly to tail. Both hind legs contorted at odd angles. And though the two front legs kept running in the air, he knew she wasn't headed to any place other than her death.

He brought his cold hands to his mouth and blew.

"Looks like we fucked each other up pretty good."

He stood up and left her and labored all the way back to the Firebird. He opened the passenger door and grabbed his black leather coat from the backseat and slipped his arms into the sleeves to hurry along some warmth. Then he bent inside again and snatched the Colt that had been flung out of the open glovebox to the floorboard.

He again clamored up the wet weedy ditch, again paced across the road, again strode to the broken doe, and again saw her impending death. He cocked a bullet into the Colt's chamber and stretched the pistol from his hand. His cold finger squeezed the trigger and the blast from the barrel sent a haunting reverberation throughout the woods that sounded like a burst of thunder hurled by a vengeful god.

2

THE HUNTER HAD BEEN TRACKING through the woods of Osage
Bend for the last three hours of night. Dressed in camouflage and veiled by darkness, his only presence had been his
heavy boots crunching across the dead leaves and broken
twigs, but as the sun was now breaking over a distant ridge,
his crystal gray eyes and his bramble of black beard were
blossoming into view.

As he snaked between lichen-spotted oaks and evergreen
pines, he spotted a young conifer with its rough brown bark
scraped away. Its naked wood flashed him like a girl's fleshy
thigh. Idling closer to it, he noticed fresh scat on the fallen
pine needles. Then a cloven hoof print sank into the soil.

Straight away, he knew it was the monster buck. Thrice
before he'd seen the twelve-pointer. The last time six weeks
ago. Its summer velvet freshly shed from its stony rack. It
had since vanished to its hidden lair, wary of predators, as it
had done so during its five-year reign in this ancient king-
dom. Still, the hunter knew the cagey old buck would be
venturing out once the first frosts of fall bit the ground. He

knew it was dutifully bound to mark the boundaries of its woodland province. Bound to battle against its rivals. Bound to charm its harem for another breed.

While he stood there and mused about the wild ways and rituals of the monster buck, his ears caught the *caw caw caw* of a crow from the hazy sky. He distrusted the black bird. Loathed its laugh. And it wasn't until its devilish cackling had disappeared through the leafless branches that he released his fear and crept on.

He trudged along the rim of the timbered peaks for another half-mile. Then he turned and pedaled downward into a vast hollow that lay between the crowded wooded hills. He came to a wide wash of rock and mud, furrowed by recent rains, and hopped over a tiny trickle of water streaming through its pebbled bed.

He followed alongside the narrow creekbed until he came upon a small clearing, and there he saw a worn-out car tire. A half-block of salt sat inside its ring.

He went toward it and bent down and ran his gloved fingers over the prints of creatures that had come by for a tasty lick. Possum. Coon. Elusive bobcat. More hoof markings of the monster buck, along with three of its devoted does.

He stood and spat into the leaves. His crystal gray eyes penetrated through the foggy woods. Searching the hillside. They arrested on a black oak with a ladder of short boards nailed onto its trunk.

He started toward it and at the end of the hundred-steps incline, his sight rolled up the black oak's trunk to see the shoddy-built deer-blind hanging in its lower branches. It looked like a pitiable treehouse left unassembled. A platform of weathered planks with no roof or no walls of any kind.

He stood for a moment longer. Contemplating. Rubbing

his bearded jaw. Then he positioned his right foot on the bottom short board and up he climbed like a clumsy bear.

It took him a couple of harrowing minutes to conquer the ascent. He then rested another before hauling himself onto the groaning boards. He carefully stayed on his hands and knees before ever-so-gingerly rolling up onto his feet. He bounced his weight upon the olden wood to ensure the floor would hold him.

Once he trusted the boards weren't going to crack, he reached inside his coveralls and out came a pint bottle of Ten High whiskey. Three times he swigged. He then groped to his hindside pocket and slid out a Redfield rifle scope and stuck it to his right eye.

The 3-9x40 magnification cut sideways in a fast-moving blur though the leafless branches of trees and trees and trees. The crosshairs then stuck hard on the salt block and worn-out tire.

He backed the scope away from his face. He swigged from the bottle once more. His mind began to envision the killing to come. Every detail of how he was going to gun down his trophy on opening day. And as he kept replaying the fated hunt over and over inside his head, a sudden dizzy spell overtook him.

His stomach wrenched. He stumbled to his knees. His head jutted over the groaning boards and the rank fluid poured out, cascading down like a shower of tainted rain.

After his stomach had drained, he turned over onto his back and breathed. He stayed quiet and still, allowing the breeze to grant him a cool reprieve, and just as it seemed that his sickness had subsided, a murder of crows cackled from somewhere unseen.

He clapped his hands over his ears and his body began

to tremble. This time he took them not to be the black birds that he so much reviled, but rather he believed they were the evil spirits coming to taunt him again.

Haints, his insane mother had called them.

Satan's spawn that preyed upon the drunk and crazy.

And since he was a daily drunk and fast becoming as insane as his insane mother had been, the evil haints had been calling more of late. He had been catching glimpses of their horned shadows. Been feeling their spiky claws sinking deeper into his brain. Now here he was hearing their heckling in these dark ancient woods, which until recently had been his sole sanctuary from his most horrible fears.

3

THE FIREBIRD'S REAR TIRES SPUN viciously on the dewy weeds, slinging a rooster plume of dirt and rocks.

The driver let off the gas. He hopped out of the car to assess the progress and found two deep sunken ruts the rubber had carved into the mud.

"God damnit!"

He turned away from his black beauty, not wanting to take his hot temper out on it, and he started kicking his boot heel into the wet ground.

"Fuck! Fuck! Fuck! Fuck!"

He huffed and rolled his eyes about the ghostly environs. Nothing but bare trees rising out of the earth like a legion of hardened Goliaths. Then another memory suddenly came back to him. This was the same stretch of desolate highway that he had once taken his daddy's prized '65 Mustang on a hell-on-wheels joyride.

He was fourteen at the time. His best friend, Byron Tisdale, was with him. The two had come up with the wily idea to hotwire the hotrod, just to see if they could, and after they got the motor purring, it was only natural that they go for a spin.

At first, they'd smartly kept the speed slow, staying on alleyways and side streets of town, avoiding notice. But once their youthful confidence had built up to full steam, they hit the curvy hills of the highway and pushed the speed. Course neither one of them expected to come upon a state trooper, and as soon as the red cherry lights spun around in pursuit, Byron hooted to *go-go-go*.

The memory brought him a whimsical grin. No doubt it had been a dimwit move he'd made as a callow kid, yet he still remained proud, even now as man, that he had given that smokey bear one hell of a chase till the rear tire of the Mustang blew. His mind was still able to picture the pissed-off smirk on the trooper's face when the copper stepped up to the car window to find two snickering boys. But then the memory brought to bear how his rotten daddy had come home drunk that night and had broken his right forearm as a fitting punishment for taking the prized Mustang.

Just then his ears perked to the distant hum of a motor. He hurried up the ditch and jogged to the center of the road. Two dim headlights shined though the fog and the boxy shape of a white Ford shortbed crawled into view.

As the truck got close, it pulled off to the side of the road. Then the window came down to reveal the prying face of an old-timer with a white beard stained blackish around his mouth.

"Hidy do," the man spoke in a friendly twang.

"Not too good right now," the driver replied, huffing complaint. "Think maybe you can pull me up out of this damn ditch?"

The old-timer squinted through his wire-rim specs and

studied the ass end of the black muscle car sticking up from the ravine. He licked his bottom lip with great thought.

"Welp, you gotta chain? Or strong rope?"

"No sir, I don't."

"Welp, we ain't gonna get very far then."

The old-timer scrutinized the brownish tinge on the driver's stubbly face and figured he must've come from the sunnier west. Still the old man's sharp ear could perceive the native tongue of a man bred in these hilly parts.

"I can give you a lift to the fillin' station if you like. They got a tow truck."

The driver gritted his teeth and again looked at his ensnared black beauty in the ditch.

"I don't reckon nobody's gonna steal it," the old man said. "Lessen they got a tow truck theyselves."

The driver tried to grin, but it broke before it rose.

"How'd you get yourself down in there?"

"Goddamn deer ran out in front of me."

"Been known to happen. Buck?"

"Doe. It's over there on the other side of the road."

"You mightta had a bit of luck with a buck. Huntin' season opens this Saturday. Tom Wrobleski, the taxidermist is havin' hisself a contest. Best rack wins a free mount and two hundred dollars, I believe it is."

"Might've helped pay for the dent in the hood." This time the driver's grin curled a bit when he tried.

The old-timer opened the truck door and stepped out. He was wearing striped denim overalls and a blue wool shirt and work boots. "Virgil Stout." He offered his hand. "Own the sportin' goods store in town."

"Thought that's who you were," the driver acknowledged,

clutching the handshake. "I used to go to your store to buy candy bars and sodas when I's a kid."

"Don't say? What be your name?"

"Pen Cullen."

"Cullen. . .?" Virgil worked his hairy jaw with his hand. "I know of a Greg Cullen. Passed on not too long back?"

The driver nodded and looked away.

"Stroke, wudn't it?"

"You'd know better than me. Hadn't see him alive for goin' on twelve, thirteen years."

Virgil's sparkling blue eyes stared at the driver, trying to figure out what his family troubles might be. But he politely decided not to intrude further.

The driver kept looking off down the road. Still nothing but gray fog and miles of towering bare trees.

"Don't look like nobody else is comin' too soon."

"Usually not this early in the mornin," Virgil confirmed, taking out a pack of chewing tobacco from the front pocket of his overalls. "Care for a chaw?"

"No thanks. I like to burn mine."

Virgil pinched off a sticky wad with his fingers and poked it inside his cheek. "Looks kinda like that Smokey and the Bandit rig you got there. Pontiac, ain't it?"

"Yeah. Except that's a Formula."

"A what?"

"Formula. Both of them's Firebirds, except that one there's a Formula. One in the movie is a Trans Am."

"Didn't know there's a difference."

"Not much of one, really."

"That sheriff sure was a pisser, wudn't he? Buford T. Justice."

The driver tightened his lips, pressing another thin grin

that couldn't quite stretch. He did not like the idea of leaving his black beauty behind, but neither was he enjoying movie talk with a goofy old hillbilly in this damn cold wind.

"I guess I better take you up on that ride."

"I'd say it's your best bet."

"Let me go get my keys."

"I ain't in no awful hurry."

The driver trotted back down to the Firebird and grabbed the keys from the ignition. He moved around to the trunk and popped the lid open to take out a stuffed duffle bag. After slamming the trunk shut, he stepped to the passenger side to lock the door. He saw the Colt .45 on the seat. His eyes peered up to the road to make sure the old-timer wasn't watching him then he slyly reached for the pistol and shoved it inside the duffle.

On the ride into town the two men stayed clammed-up toward one another, other than Virgil humming along with Porter and Dolly crooning on the AM radio. Pen mostly stared out the window, rubbing his knuckles into his eye sockets, replaying the all-night hell-ride he'd been on. It was about six o'clock last night when he had checked-out from a low rent motel in Tucumcari, right before the western sky had purpled and dotted itself with desert starlight. After escaping the pink alabaster dunes of New Mexico, he had driven through the lean panhandle of West Texas, across the red dirt flatlands of Oklahoma, and into the knotty mountains of Arkansas. His last stop had been four hours ago near the little town of Flippin where he had pulled into a truck stop for gas and coffee.

"You care if I have a smoke?"

"Why no, go right ahead."

Pen lit up a Camel and cracked the window.

"Hellacious weather we been havin', ain't it?"

"I live in the desert," Pen obliged a response. "Weather don't change much."

"Oh yeah, where's that?"

"Nevada."

"Don't say? Ain't never made it no further west than Kansas myself. Nice out there?"

"If you like snakes and lizards."

"Well, it sure ain't been dry here. Weather's been as moody as an old gal who's dropped her sex parts. One day she's full of sunshine, next day she's rippin' thunder. The damned rain this spring and summer was like somethin' I ain't never seen. Came down so strong it damn near flooded every town along both the Mississippi and Missouri Rivers. Got a grandson up in Jeff City lost his house, his truck, his dogs. About everythin' else he owned. Says he wished it'd took his wife."

Virgil grinned at his own joke and spit a mouthful of tobacco juice into a stained coffee cup.

"He fenced his yard about four-foot high with sandbags, course that didn't hold worth a lick when that ole muddy river water came a rushin' down like it was the end of times. Warshed everything downstream quick as shit from a race mare's puckered ass. I reckon no man can impede the Almighty's wrath once it comes. Just gotta hold on and pray that it ain't your time to go."

"I think I saw somethin' about it on the news," Pen replied, trying to be cordial to the old-timer's babbling.

"Still feel right terrible for him. He's had a hard go of it. Harder than most anyways. He'd been over there in Kuwait givin' that Saddam bastard some country boy hell. He took a metal piece to his head. Scarred his face a bit and lost two fingers on his right hand. Then this damn flood came down on him. Makes me wonder how much more the boy's gotta take before somethin' good comes along."

Pen wordlessly agreed to the old-timer's wonderment over mankind's tragic fates, though he was thinking more of his own wretched path. As his cigarette smoke curled out the window, he spotted a sun-bleached billboard with its flaked words scarcely visible by the shedding paint.

Doe Run, Missouri – On the Leading Edge of Progress!

"Don't look like things have changed much."

"Doe Run's never been much more than a speck of fly shit on a slaughterhouse wall." Virgil chortled. "Still a decent place for most God-fearin' folks."

They came upon Jessup Brothers gas station. Pen halfway expected to see Jim Jessup perched on the bench outside. He remembered how back in earlier years, old man Jessup would be sitting on that bench with a big beam on his face, handing out free bubble gum to all the folks driving in for a fill-up. But those days were long gone. Jim Jessup and his three brothers were either dead or retired, and nothing came for no-cost anymore, including grins and gum.

They pulled into the lot and parked and hopped out. Pen peeled his sights over the piles of grimy car parts scattered around. He figured organized neatness must have died with Jim Jessup too. He flicked the butt of his Camel onto the cement and followed Virgil toward the station door.

Inside, a greasy-clothed and greasy-haired station attendant stood behind the counter, browsing the sticky pages of a porn magazine, and he jumped when a bell jingled above the opening door.

"How do, Wayne," Virgil announced.

The attendant shoved his girly rag into a drawer. "Morin' Virgil," he replied, casting a yellow-teeth grin.

"This fella here's got his car stuck in a ditch, about eight miles down T highway and needs a tow."

"Well Junior's done gone out with the truck."

"This early?"

"Everett Caldwell called up last night," Wayne nodded, "said his John Deere rolled down a hill and into his pond. Junior headed out first thing this mornin' to pull 'er out."

Virgil glanced at Pen. "Ain't in no hurry, are you?"

Pen peered up at the Busch beer logo clock on the wall which showed the time of 7:10.

"You know what time the bank opens?"

"Nine sharp I believe," Virgil answered.

Pen blew air through his lips. "Guess I got some time to kill." He then strolled over to the coffee pot in the corner of the room and poured a large to-go cup.

Wayne watched the stranger closely, curious over who he might be, and raised his highbrows toward Virgil.

"He kissed a deer on his way into town," Virgil whispered. "Left quite a mark on the car hood from what he says."

"Buck?"

"Doe."

Pen sauntered back to the counter with his coffee in hand and placed it down. "I'll take a carton of Camel filters and a couple packs of Levi Garrett for Mr. Stout here."

"Aww, there's no need for that."

Pen withdrew a twenty from his wallet and slid it across

the counter. "You didn't come along and hitch me a ride, I might still be out there cuppin' my frozen nuts."

"Well, all right then, I won't turn you down twice." Virgil nodded kindly. "Anywhere else you need to get to?"

"Don't know where it'd be," Pen answered, shrugging. "Sort of lost touch."

"With who?" Wayne pried.

Pen looked down and tapped the point of his boot against the bottom of the counter, not wishing to remember anyone. "Well, I used to hang with a guy named Byron Tisdale."

Virgil and Wayne exchanged glances with one another.

"Byron's still around, far as I know," Wayne replied with a lilt voice. "But I ain't seen much of him since that mess happened with his kid."

Pen's eyes shifted between them, waiting for either man to spit it out.

"What mess is that?"

"You ain't heard it?"

"Guess not."

"About a year and a half back," Virgil started, "there's a sum bitch livin' out on the west side of town, Sam Groat's his name. He up and killed Byron's little boy."

Pen's eyes widened. "On purpose?"

"That depends on who's tellin' it." Virgil glanced down to his shuffling feet. "Law said it was an accident."

"Aw hell Virgil, everybody knowed it wasn't no goddamn accident," Wayne piped up. "You knowed it, I knowed it, everybody knowed it."

"I only know Sam Groat's an odd bird and he'll answer for his ways one turn or another."

"The law should of throwed that son of bitch in jail and tossed away the goddamn key," Wayne shot out. "You tell me how in hell somebody can just up and shoot a boy like that and not pay for it--?"

"--I'm sayin' I don't know the whole of it, so don't be puttin' me in the same poke of folks who think they do," Virgil snapped back. "Some things just can't be understood and that's all there is to it."

Wayne quieted then nodded an apology. "Just gets me riled whenever I think about it."

Pen sipped his coffee.

"Sounds like I have missed out on a few things."

4

THE KILLING OF JACOB TISDALE took place at half-past midnight on July 9, 1991, in the yard of Sam Groat's house on D Highway. The weapon used was a Savage Model 30 twelve-gauge pump-action shotgun, which had discharged three loads of #4 buckshot. Those were the facts everyone could pretty much agree upon. But the rest of the grisly tale was left up to witness testimonies, a police investigation, rumors, a trial, and a whole lot of varying opinions about the character of the man who pulled the trigger.

The most accepted version began when ten-year-old Jacob Tisdale was spending the night at the home of another ten-year-old boy by the name of Ricky Vaughn. The Vaughn residence was also on D Highway. Ricky's mother, Lisa Vaughn, explained on the witness stand that she had sent the two boys off to bed at around ten-thirty that night, and she had looked in Ricky's bedroom at eleven to make sure they were tucked in. She said they were. And she also said that neither she or her husband, Bobby Vaughn, had any way of knowing that the two boys were going to sneak out of the house at midnight.

Apparently, Ricky and Jacob had designed their adventure earlier that afternoon when they were shooting pellet guns at sparrows in the barn. Ricky testified that they had planned to slip out of the house after his parents went to bed, and then they were going to hike across the neighboring fields with their flashlights until they reached Angie Groat's house less than a mile away. Angie was a friend of theirs from school and the boys thought it would be funny to scare her. So sure enough, when midnight arrived and the two boys saw that the light in the bedroom of Ricky's parents had gone out, they snuck down the stairs and went out the kitchen door.

Ricky said that because they had walked over the same route many times before in daytime, they already knew the best places to duck under the barbwire fences, and their only real worry was Sam Groat's nasty Hereford bull that had charged at them a couple times before. But Ricky said they never did see the Hereford bull or any cattle at all that night.

According to the investigation it must have taken the boys a little over a half hour to make it to the Groat residence. Ricky said when they got a few hundred yards away from the electric pole light that illuminated the yard, they shut off their flashlights and held in their snickers to not be heard. Both boys knew which window belonged to Angie's bedroom, as they'd both been inside the house before, and after they heartened their mischievous courage, they hunkered down and scampered across the yard.

Once they had made it to Angie's window, Ricky said that he reached up and scratched his fingernails across the screen and it made a swishing noise. The kind of sound that sometimes makes people grow goosebumps on their skin. Ricky said they waited a minute or so, and then Jacob reached up and did the same thing. Then they each took turns doing it again and again, about five or six times, all the while believing that Angie would start screaming and then they would run all the way back home like they had planned.

But what the two boys didn't realize, and there was probably not a way they could have, was that Angie had been awake the whole time. She told the court that she was scared sure enough. How could she not be? But instead of screaming out loud, she jumped out of bed and hurried out the bedroom to tell her daddy that something scary was outside.

Now whether the rest of this particular version of the story of that tragic night is truthful or not depends largely on whether you can trust the words of Angie's daddy, Sam Groat, or whether you can trust the words of ten-year-old Ricky, who was so damn frightened that he might not have even seen what really happened. Either way, what happened did happen.

Sam claimed that he was watching a rerun of *MASH* in the living room when his little girl came running in and told him something was making a racket on her window. At the trial, Angie backed up her daddy's testimony, and she added that her body was shaking from fear when she told him about the noise, so nobody has ever argued whether or not there was at least a certain degree of worry involved. But what had been disputed, even before that deadly night, was Sam Groat's nature and his predilection for orneriness. It was no fantastic secret that Sam had always been a private sort. His father was a private man, and his granddaddy had been the same, so it just came with the Groat family gene. And besides, being a private sort had never been an uncommon trait for most generations living in the Ozark hills, both past and present. That said, a man's God-given right to privacy was one thing, but his temperament was another matter. And a whole lot of folks around these parts believed that Sam Groat possessed enough of a mean streak inside of him to do almost anything violent. Some even claimed Sam only kept that nasty Hereford bull to warn folks off his pastures because that damn nasty Hereford bull sure wasn't worth its price in siring calves. To them, that damn nasty bull merely represented the kind of black heart beating in Sam Groat's chest.

Another side of Sam Groat's nature was marked by his preference to tuck away either a shotgun or a rifle in places all around his house just in case he ever needed them. Though he had never told anyone what exact need he had in mind. So back on that tragic night on July 9th, he had gone straight for the family heirloom Savage 30 pump that he kept inside the closet nearest to the front door. He had also made certain that a ready-to-go buckshot load was in its chamber before he crept quietly through the house and out the back.

During the trial, Sam swore on a Holy Bible that he'd thought the scratching sound coming from his little girl's window was probably nothing more than a coon looking for table scraps. But when he came around the corner of the house and caught sight of two shadowy figures standing under Angie's bedroom window, he claimed that he got scared for his life. He also maintained that he had given the shadowy figures fair enough warning to not move, but one of them, little Ricky as it had later found out to be, took off across the yard at a dead sprint and was gone before Sam could do anything about it.

On the witness stand, Ricky didn't disagree with what

Sam Groat had testified. Ricky confessed that he took off running right when he saw Sam Groat come around the corner of the house. But he added that he'd hollered for Jacob to run with him. And as the police investigation had verified, Jacob did run, except he ran in a different direction than Ricky. For some reason, almost certainly the little boy's sheer fright, Jacob had darted toward a row of hedge apple trees standing about a hundred yards from the house, the same trees which had been planted there by Sam himself thirty years ago as a windbreak, and when Jacob made it to those trees, he crouched down and hid instead of running back to Ricky's house like they had planned to do.

Sam declared over and over that he'd honestly believed the shadowy figures he had seen in his yard were a threat to him and his family, and if anyone else had been standing in his boots that night, with a Savage shotgun in hand, then he reckoned they probably would've done the same thing as he had. On the other hand, Sam did not once give any impressive answers to the judge and jury as to why he'd been so foolhardy to chase after such a so-called threat. Another unanswered question was why Sam hadn't recognized Ricky's screams as coming from the high-pitched squeal of a scared little boy. But most puzzling of all was the unanswered question of why Sam had chosen to fire three loads of #4 buckshot, at a distance of eight feet, directly and purposely into the face of a ten-year-old boy named Jacob Tisdale.

Whatever the true tale might have been that night, the second-degree manslaughter trial of Sam Groat ended with a hung jury of nine guilty against three not guilty. The lack of a verdict didn't stomach too well with a whole lot of folks in town. Some felt the entire incident was a tragedy in and of itself, and the little boy probably shouldn't have been playing mischief. Yet some others resented the fact that Sam Groat would still be walking this earth as a free man. To the latter folks, Sam Groat might have had his God-given right to his privacy, but that goddamn mean streak living inside of him needed to pay some sort of price for what he had done.

5

PEN STOOD BEFORE THE RUST-STAINED SINK inside the men's room and washed the doe's death off his hands. His strained eyes gravitated to the corroded mirror and the familiar face he saw in its warped reflection seemed more aged than its thirty-one years. He leaned closer into the distorted likeness of himself and spotted crows-feet scratching near his lids and a couple of gray hairs poking from his black brows, and he could almost swear that he was looking right in the eyes of his rotten daddy.

He yanked himself from the mirror and rifled through his duffle and out came a pill bottle. He dumped the last two white-cross speed tablets into his palm and shoveled them down his throat with a handful of running water. Then he grabbed a handful of coarse paper towels and vigorously swabbed his wet face, peeping at the mirror again to make sure his rotten daddy wasn't looking back at him.

When he came out of the men's room, Wayne was still standing behind the counter, casting his yellow-teeth grin.

"Should have your car here in a couple hours."

Pen checked the time on the Busch logo clock. 7:20.

"Guess I'll be back about that time then."

He headed for the door without another word and when he strode outside, Virgil was there waiting for him, propped against the front of the shortbed Ford. The old-timer leaned up and spit a mouthful of brown juice onto the cement.

"Sure you don't need a ride somewheres else?"

Pen tugged the strap of his duffle onto his shoulder and squinted in the direction of where he thought he might go.

"Naw, I'm good. Think I'll take a little walk, see what I've been missin.'"

Virgil shuffled his feet in a stoic posture. "You know, I just thought of it, but if you wanna track down Byron Tisdale, you might stop by the Queenway Diner. His wife waitresses there. I see her most mornin's I stop by to shoot the bull with the fellers I know go regular."

Pen's attention spun back around to the old man as if he'd heard a siren's wail.

"What's her name?"

"Tara."

"Tara Hawkins?"

"Believe that's her maiden name. You know her?"

"Used to," Pen whispered, nodding.

"Believe they been split up for a spell. But she might know where he's keepin' hisself."

Pen ran his hand over whiskered cheeks. Struggling to believe.

Virgil waited for more elaboration, but it didn't come. He blew the wet wad of Levi Garrett out of his mouth.

"Well alright, I best get the store."

"Thanks again for the ride," Pen uttered, trying to take back hold of his shattered self.

"Just the Christian thing to do. Welcome home."

By seven forty-five, the denizens of Doe Run were waking to the brisk November day. Mud-splattered 4x4's and dually pickups were rumbling along, piloted by hard-face bearded men smoking cigarettes or biting chaw. Blue Bird school buses were grinding their gears down the streets, with the white flat noses of playful children pressed against the fogged windows. Staggered herds of walking-to-school broods were bundled up in their colorful coats and knit hats, while a few others were racing on their squeaky BMX bikes.

Pen was striding on the sidewalks among them, taking in the sights and sounds, hands balled into his pockets and the duffle slung over his shoulder. Frozen within his curious wonder over the news of Tara Hawkins and Byron Tisdale.

Married.

With a dead kid between them.

His eyes roved to the screened porch houses that he remembered from years ago, noting the slight variations of the same color paint slapped over previous coats, or a chain fence squared around a yard, or new shingles on a roof. With only a hundred or so buildings in town, including the wood-frame town hall, he got the sense that Doe Run was still nothing more than a podunk shithole polluted by head-strong ignorance and stubborn pride.

He soon came to the three-block commerce section of town, and he stopped to survey the century-old vernacular buildings made of red clay bricks and limestone. Johnson's Hardware. Bennington's Furniture. Sandy's Boutique. Willard's Barbershop. Bowles Drugstore. Williams Meat house. Hamblin's Feedlot. Roy's Insurance. Nothing had changed much except maybe the brands or styles of wares they sold. However, he was amused to see stop signs posted at every cross street. Doe Run sure enough appeared to be on the leading edge of progress.

He walked on and took a left turn on Broadway. Two blocks down he strolled across a one-lane bridge and halted midway to light a Camel. He peered over the railing to see the running creek below. Maybe three-foot. Roughly a foot lower than the great flood of '76. He remembered how the procession of thunderstorms that year had put the town underwater, and how the planned Bicentennial fireworks didn't boom until October.

As he stood there and smoked and recalled days of yonder, he saw a mangy collie jet out from underneath the bridge. Then came two boys, around twelve, hot on her trail and chucking stones. When the bitch caught one on the spine she yelped in a high pitch and her backend hunkered down.

"I got it!" the larger of the two boys hollered.

Then the smaller one cocked his arm and let another sail.

"Hey there," Pen called down. "Leave that dog alone."

The boys stopped and looked up at the brooding stranger standing on the bridge. Guilt poured out of their open mouths.

"Just a stray," the larger one replied, half-grinning. "She don't belong to nobody."

"That give you a right to throw rocks at her?"

The boys gaped at one another, still slack-jawed, waiting for the other one to say something defiant.

"You two better let that dog alone," Pen advised them. "You don't, I might have to come down there and make it two on two."

The stray bitch had stopped running on the other side

of the muddy creek bank, and she was now peering back at the man standing upon the bridge. Her matted and cockle-burred tail wasn't wagging, so it was hard to tell if she was thankful to him or not. More like she was judging if his soul was tainted or pure.

The two delinquents glanced at each other again, still neither one daring to argue back.

"Can we have a cigarette?" asked the larger one.

"Why don't y'all get yourselves on to school."

"That mean you won't give us one?"

"It means I'm tired of talkin' to you. Now go on."

As the two sulking boys headed back in the direction from where they had come, Pen's mind floated back to when he was their age. Unpredictable. Full of mischief. He guessed that it must be something in the countrified air that made boys in this town so rowdy and malicious, and there was nothing he could have ever done to change how he'd turned out to be.

His mind began to recall the time back in fourth grade when he and Byron first became buddies. He and the other elementary boys would gather on the playground at recess for a roughhouse game called Smear the Queer. The only rules to it involved punting a rubber kicking ball into the air and the player who happened to catch it--recognized as the queer--had to run like hell before everyone else chased and pummeled him to the ground. It was sort of like wildborn pups honing their kill skills with one another outside the den. For the most part the boys played pretty fair and no one got marred too awful, other than whelps and bruises and occasional busted lips. However, one day a smartass bigger kid named Kenny Pruitt started getting a little too rough with the smaller boys. He was slamming them from behind and elbowing them in the ribs, and he would just snort a laugh whenever they cried foul. Pen disregarded Kenny's bully act as best he could and justly took his turns catching the ball and tackling the different queers. But when he witnessed Kenny purposely trip a blameless girl who was only watching the boys play, his ire set in, and with no advance warning he snatched the ball out of the air and forcefully hurled it straight into Kenny's face.

The impact was brutal. The big bully fell to his knees and covered his stung nose with his hands and started bawling. As the other boys gathered around, anxious to see a scrap, Pen glared insult and shouted for Kenny to stop blubbering and take his fair medicine. It should've ended there. But because Kenny was not the sort who could hold his smartass mouth shut, he irately started to spout mean and nasty words. Vile words, like how Pen's mom had croaked just to get out of raising such a shithead son.

Pen rushed forward to knock the snot out of the bastard bully, but before he had the chance, the fat kid everyone called Spook unexpectedly spun out from the crowd and blindsided Kenny in the jaw. Spook followed up with a volley of vicious slugs about Kenny's face, his fists flying so fast that all of the other kids could only gape in stunned shock, and if Pen had not pulled Spook away from Kenny, then everyone there might've witnessed a real-life murder at recess that day.

The outcome was predictable. Pen and Spook were each whipped five licks by the principal's paddle. Smartass Kenny Pruitt would have received the same if it had not been for his cracked cheek bone and swollen lips. Then three days after the violent ruckus, the school board unanimously voted to send Spook away to a juvenile reform school until he could abide by the common rules of civility. Still, even after all the penalties had been dealt, and Smear the Queer had been forever banished from school, no one had any idea why Spook had jumped into the fracas like he'd done. Including, Pen. It wasn't like he and Spook were friends looking out for one another. In fact, they'd met in a couple of shoving matches in their earlier grades that had nearly led to fist shots.

The motives for Spook's violent actions remained a mystery until the following year in fifth grade when he was permitted to return to elementary school. One day during lunchtime, Pen walked up behind him in the cafeteria line and flat-out asked him why he had whipped Kenny Pruitt's ass like he'd done. Spook took a moment before his voice broke. He said that Kenny shouldn't have spouted those mean words. Then he admitted that he got pissed whenever he heard kids say mean words about his own momma. Mean words like how she wore a motorcycle helmet whenever she drove a car. How she had once danced through the neighborhood wearing nothing but her pantyhose and bra. How she would buy an entire shelf of creamed corn at the grocery store from time to time for no sound reason. Yet Spook believed the meanest words of all were the whispered claims that his grandfolks were brother and sister, and so his momma was an inbred. He admitted that his momma might act a little different than others, but she was still his momma, and there was not another woman in this whole wide world better than she. Judging by the teardrops forming in Spook's crystal gray eyes, Pen recognized the fat kid was speaking from the heart, and from that day forward they became as tight as a pair of strings on a broken harp. And never again did Pen refer to his new friend as Spook.

As the burned-down stub of the Camel dropped down

from the bridge and fell into the running water, Pen's child-hood recollections of Byron Tisdale floated away with it. He gazed up to notice the collie bitch was still standing across the way. Still judging him. He didn't like the feeling of being observed, even by a damn bitch dog, so he turned and peered down Broadway Street. The Queenway Diner sign flashed three blocks away. He wondered if Tara Hawkins was there. Then he wondered what he was going to say to her if she was.

6

THE QUEENWAY WAS LIVELY this morning with its general crowd of scruffy-bearded sawmillers, grease-stained loggers, and gray-hair farmers with their overweight farmer sons. All of them working their mouths on novel lies and cheap cigarettes, and wearing some combination of faded flannel shirt, wool-lined coat, dingy cap, and marred boots.

A pack of ten such yahoos were clumped together in the far back corner table. They had just polished off their morning diet of runny eggs, burnt bacon, and hash browns, and were now patting their stuffed bellies as their comely waitress threaded through them, refilling their coffee mugs and clearing their empty plates. She purposely avoided looking any man in the face, as she loathed their roving and predatory eyes. Even more, she hated their perverted jokes aimed her way. Like what a damn shame it was to see such a fine piece of ass wasting on the vine.

"John Kuntz was bow hunting yesterday afternoon out by Crowley's Ridge," uttered one of the nasty men, named Pete, "and claims he saw a sixteen pointer."

"Bullshit if he ain't lyin," replied portly Charlie Johnson, sitting staunch at the head of the table.

"Did he get a shot at it?" another man piped in.

"Five times," he says. But it never came no closer than seventy, eighty yards. Says it just stood there and looked around at what the hell these arrows were fallin' from the sky."

"Well, how'd he know it's a sixteen pointer if he didn't get no closer than 'at?" Charlie inquired, still holding his doubt.

"Binoculars, I reckon."

"By gawd if that's the holy book's truth, ye can bet your high-ass dollar I'm gonna be out there Saturday mornin' with my thirty-thirty," another man named Bill claimed.

"Shit Bill, I seen you shoot," said another man in the group, winking. "If that ole buck don't get no closer than seventy yards, it ain't gonna make a damn difference if you got a cannon or slingshot."

"Well, you ain't seen me shoot in a while," retorted Bill. "I been practicin."

"With your rifle or pee gun?" Pete blurted out. "From what I hear tell from your wife, your needin' to work on your aim."

All the nasty men guffawed at Bill's expense. Even Bill himself had to laugh at that one before adding, "Was she gripin' about me goin' through her back barn door again?"

The entire table of men nearly fell out of their seats, howling. After the outburst subsided, Charlie reached his mug out for the waitress to refill it and carried on with his recent deer hunting assertions. "Well, I don't know if ole John was stretchin' the truth or not, but my brother-in-law's got a place picked out over in Howell County. Says there's a few bucks worth the time, but most are thinner than a sawhorse on account of the soybeans bein' flooded out this summer."

As the waitress leaned closer to Charlie's coffee mug, her sight fixed on the customer who just passed into the doorway and a jolt of surprise shook through her bones.

"Hot damn! Hot damn!!" Charlie mercifully cried, shaking the sizzling black liquid off his fingers.

"Oh, my goodness," the waitress whined, jerking up the coffee pot before it spilled more on him.

"Shit. Shit. Shit that burns."

"I'm so sorry Mr. Johnson," she apologized, trying to mop his hands with paper napkins.

"Damn Tara, you done scalded Charlie's trigger hand," Pete added, snickering. "Now he's gonna have a verifiable excuse for his piss poor shootin' come Saturday."

As the men kept chuckling at Charlie's expense, Pen stood stuck at the doorway and assessed how Tara Hawkins had grown up. Her long straight hair that she used to whip into a ponytail was now cropped off at her shoulders and it shone more of a lighter chestnut color rather than dark coffee brown. She'd put on maybe ten-to-twelve pounds. Even so she still looked slender and firm in that goofy-ass waitress uniform, and if anything, those few extra pounds had put a nice curve into her swish.

Embarrassed and shied by the stranger standing at the door, Tara whisked across the dining room, plates and coffee pot in her hands. With each footstep, her eyes nervously shifted toward and away at him, and she could only bring herself to mutter, "Seat yourself wherever you like," as she rambled by.

Once she made it to the counter and set down the stack of plates and the coffee pot, she felt a ripple of puke rising from her stomach. She peeped over to a fellow waitress who was busy balancing hot plates of food onto her arms.

"Stephanie, can you watch my tables for a minute?"

"Right now?"

"I think I'm gonna be sick."

And away she went.

Tara made it to the back of the kitchen and rushed inside the worker's restroom. After locking the door, she went straight for the sink and spun on the knob. She slapped cool water onto her flushed forehead and cheeks, and then she looked into the mirror and saw a reflection of shame and upheaval.

Pen sat at a small table by the window. The white-crosses had kicked in and killed his appetite, he could only nibble at his plate of biscuits and gravy. Between sips of coffee, he kept looking over his shoulder, ponderous over Tara's abrupt disappearance. She hadn't shown herself since she gave her curt reception to him at the door and he was beginning to resent coming here. She didn't even seem to recognize who he was.

Stephanie sauntered up with a coffee pot and leered down at him like a barn cat ready to paw a field mouse.

"Refill your coffee, darlin'?"

He pushed his cup across the table. "Won't turn you down."

"Have I seen you in here before?"

"It's possible. But not likely." He watched the steaming pour from her pot into his cup. "Pretty busy. You the only waitress?"

"Only one workin' it appears," Stephanie smirked, her eyes rolling toward the kitchen.

Pen raised his cup up at her. "Thanks."

"What I'm here for. Can I get you anything else?"

"Think I'm good."

"Well just let me know if you need anything, darlin'. I'm busy, but not too busy."

As Stephanie dragged herself away, he stole a glance at some of the local menfolk stealing a glance back at him. He didn't recognize any of them. He felt an urge to flip them the finger to see what might happen, but he fought it off by turning his eyes out the window.

Another five minutes. His coffee went cold. Then he heard a voice sing behind his back.

"Thought you were never comin' back."

His head turned from the window to see Tara standing there. She'd come with a spread of wet lipstick and a coat of rouge to frame her bright and smiley face.

His mouth formed a pearly grin. "Well, never's quite a bit of time to be considerin' much of anythin', ain't it?"

When Tara's sight fell upon his white choppers and his stubbled chin, she felt her throat drop into her chest.

"I didn't recognize you when you first came in."

"That a compliment?"

"If you want it to be."

"Still waitressin', huh?"

"It suits me." Her newborn confidence dropped a notch. "I actually just started back not too long ago. I had other things goin' on."

Pen noted her once round face had drawn thin and delicate on the bone and her skin color held a lucent gleam of a pearl.

"How long you been in town for?"

"What, you didn't hear the welcoming parade comin' down the street? Had a marchin' band and the whole shebang."

"Must've missed it."

"I just rolled in this mornin'." Now that she was in

front of him, his eyes couldn't let go of her. "Got a minute to sit?"

Tara knew she didn't have the time. She also knew everyone in the joint would gossip if she did. But the temptation was too strong to resist, so she pulled out a chair.

"Just a quick one."

She sank into the seat and they both looked into one another's faces, failing to conjure a sentence to say.

"I'm sorry," she finally stuttered in a breathy way. "It's just kind of strange seein' you."

"Look all you want. I'm real."

"Why are you here?"

"Stomach was growlin'."

"I mean in Doe Run."

He lifted his coffee mug and sipped its coldness, his eyes again catching the stares of curious customers upon them.

"I had to come and tie-up some loose ends with what the old man left behind."

"Oh. . ." Tara peered down to the table. "I went to his funeral."

He snorted in jest. "What in hell for?"

"I just felt like I should." Her fingers began to fidget with the sugar caddy. "Since he came to ours and all."

Her eyes sprang back at him, her face frozen.

"My boy's," she softly voiced.

He looked at her hands fidgeting the sugar caddy, noticing her fingernails gnawed to the quick and bleeding scabs. He decided it best not to let on that he knew about her child's death.

"How's your folks? They still teachin'?"

"Not anymore," she answered, faintly, eyes still fixed on the sugar caddy.

Stephanie stomped by them with steaming plates of pancakes and sausage in her hands, and snapped, "If you ain't still sick, think you can help me?"

Tara looked up from the table, "Be right there." Then she squared her eyes on Pen. "They retired and bought a mobile home and go all over the place with it. Mom just called a couple of days ago and said they were somewhere in Georgia at a Civil War battle site."

"No shit? Regular old snowbirds, huh?"

"I think they've gone senile," Tara sighed in jest. "But I swear, there are more times than not I wish I would've gone off with them."

"And miss bein' stuck here with all these pretty faces?" Pen nudged his chin toward the nasty men at the back table, and Tara's head went around to see Charlie and Bill's jealousy glaring at them.

"Hardly," she groaned.

"So how's Byron doin'?"

Her face came back around to him and went a bit pinkish. He too was momentarily taken aback that he'd asked it, but something in him was unable to restrain his curiosity.

"You know we was married?" she whispered, distant and pained.

"Grapevine ain't too short from the gas station to here."

"We didn't turn out to be so picture perfect, I guess you could say."

"Excuse me, Tara?" interrupted a nearby diner customer, holding up his bill. "I'm ready to pay."

"Be right there, Mr. Long," she replied, waving back.

"Know where he's at?"

"Byron? He's stayin' out on Joe Silva's farm last I heard."

"Joe's? What in hell is he doin' out there?"

Her face fell grave. "He's changed."

"Into what?" Pen huffed with a chuckle.

"He's changed, is all."

With the same grave expression not leaving her face, Tara eased up from the chair and scooted it back to the table. "I better get back to work before they start hollerin' at me."

"Yeah, I don't want to get you in trouble."

She lingered another moment with a desperate look on her face.

"How long you here for?"

"I don't know. Depends on what all I gotta do with this estate stuff."

"Well stop by again, if you can," she said softly and flustered. "Maybe I'll have more time to talk."

"Sure thing."

Then she frowned and spun around and glided off to her nosy and nasty customers.

Pen reached for a Camel and lit it. He watched her closely as smoke circled around his head, ruminating over how much Tara Hawkins had grown up from the high school girl he had once intimately known. He speculated on what might've happened to her. He could only figure that being married to Byron and the death of her child had wounded her ways in which he could not fully understand. And he also realized in that lonesome moment of studying the only woman who had ever held his heart that he could never be the same man who once called Doe Run his home.

7

A RUSTED '79 DODGE RAM pulled into the lot of Yonker's liquor store. The tiny booze house was located six miles from town and it was deserted at this early hour of day.

The engine cut off and out from the cab stepped the hunter, still clothed in his camouflage getup. He shut the truck door and craned his head from side to side, believing someone was watching him. He spat on the ground and made his way toward the store.

Ray Yonker stood behind the counter, adjusting the rabbit ears on a fuzzy screen TV, and when he heard the door squeak open, he turned to see the forlorn appearance of a thirsty man walk in.

"Mornin' Byron. Usual?"

"Yes sir."

"Aw, the hell with ya," Yonker carped, smacking the side of the TV. The fuzzy screen blinked into lines and a volume of static drowned out the audio of the morning news from Cape Girardeau. Yonker bent his head up to the shelves of liquor bottles stacked high behind the counter.

"Can you believe Slick Willie and these bellyachin' liberals are gonna make it so when you buy a gun it's gonna take five goddamn days before ya can get it?"

"I ain't been payin' no attention to it," Byron muttered, his focus on the wad of crumpled dollar bills dangling between his mud-stained fingers.

Yonker reached up and grabbed a couple of fifths and a pint of Ten High bourbon.

"That sumbitch Clinton ain't from no damn Arkansas far I can tell. Before ya know it, he'll have these Yankees tryin' to tote off with the guns we done already own."

Byron laid his money out on the counter and gawked at the whiskey bottles like an infant famished for nipple drops.

Yonker read the price tags on the bottles and rang up the sale. "Comes to twenty-four seventy-two." He counted the pile of ones and fives, sticking the bills in the register slots, then slapped twenty-eight cents change onto the counter.

Byron slid his coins into his palm and grasped the necks of the three bottles. "Thanks."

Then he headed out the door.

"Don't drink her all at once now." Yonker waved, then turned his attention back to the fuzzy screen.

When Byron got back inside the Ram, he tossed the two larger bottles onto the passenger seat, then twisted off the cap from the pint bottle and took burning swallows till it was half empty. A fiery fume of relief blew through his wetted lips when he brought the bottle back down, and his eyes shot out the windshield to make certain no haints were there.

He saw no signs of horned shadows dancing about the lot.

Didn't hear any laughter tickling his ears.

He raised the pint again and killed it. Backwash spittled out the corner of his mouth and he wiped it with his sleeve.

He checked out the windshield once more.
Both side windows.
The back glass.
Nothing there.
He tossed the empty bottle onto the floorboard and started up the truck.
Then drove away.

8

PEN STOOD ON THE SIDEWALK across the street from the Town & County Bank and tolerably waited for a semi loaded with fifty-foot cut oaks to crawl past the intersection. His eyes looked up to the bank's clock tower and read *Established in 1894* written under the present time of 9:10 AM. He then caught a passing glance at the driver of the semi, noting the craggy face with listless black eyes, and he wondered if it might be the Grim Reaper out for a morning spin.

After the back end of the log truck had cleared the way, he went on across the street with a noticeably loftier pep in his stride--thanks to the speed pills and the biscuits and gravy breakfast and the mesmerizing visit with Tara Hawkins. He strutted up to the glass double-door of the red brick bank and halted mid-step to note the business hours stenciled above the brass handles.

Monday through Friday 9:00 AM - 3:00 PM
Saturday 9:00 AM - NOON

He pulled the door open, and upon entering the lobby, his hazel eyes peeled over the entire layout of the place.

Every inch was just as he had remembered. The shiny black-and-white marble floor. The wood panel walls adorned with Rotary plaques. The dark hickory counter stationed in the middle of the lobby, still bearing the pen marks scratched by panicked customers at the start of the Depression. The plastic trees still ungrown in their soilless pots, and the knee-high brass ashtrays still filled with gray sand. The colossal crystal chandeliers hanging high in the rafters, and dangling between them the olden guard turret, fashioned there during the grand robber days of Bonny and Clyde.

His sight arrested upon two chunky secretaries at their desks, sipping mugs and munching cinnamon rolls, and near them were the glassed-walled offices of their tight-fisted bosses. His head slowly turned toward the lengthy counter of teller windows where a small cluster of early-bird customers were standing in lines. Mostly store owners, waiting alongside harping housewives and their snot-nose brats. The four women tellers working the windows were overweight chatty oafs, ranging in the middle-to-late ages. He recognized one of them as Tammy Dixon. Her line seemed the shortest, so he ambled her way and got in line behind an old witch-looking woman adorned in a black dress and black coat and black hat.

"I ain't never seen streets so busy," crowed an old witch. "It's a wonder I ain't get run over."

"Well now, it's a hectic time for everybody," Tammy kindly explained with the stick of a cherry red sucker poked out from her mouth. "Stores are just gettin' a little extra bit of business this week from the hunters comin' through."

"Well, it ain't doin' me no durn good," the old witch complained. "Ye ask me, this huntin' business ain't nothin' but a barn of horseshit."

"Now Ms. Robinson, you better watch what you're sayin' in here," Tammy warned. "You remember what happened last time."

"I ain't said nothin' terrible."

"No, but you was probably fixin' to."

"Don't ye be sassin' me none, I come here to do my business is all," the old witch scoffed. "Y'all just fortunate to be the only bank that can cash a check, otherwise ye'd be run out in feathers. Ought to be ashamed of yourselves. Stealin' from poor folks."

Tammy blew an aggravated breath then methodically counted the cash she laid out onto the counter. "Twenty, thirty, five, forty, one, two, three, and two more dollars in quarters."

Pen waited affably behind the old witch and watched her shove her bills and coins into her black leather wallet. When he got a better gander at her wrinkled walnut face and smacking toothless gums, he thought she might be the wife of the Grim Reaper he just saw outside driving the log truck.

"Now take care of yourself, Ms. Robinson," Tammy said pleasantly. "I'll see you back here again next week."

"Not if ye die first," the old witch snapped. "I curse ye. I curse ye and this whole goddamn filthy bank."

She then turned her attention toward Pen and the dumbstruck customers. "I curse ye, I curse ye," she kept going, pointing her boney finger at them, until she whisked herself out the door.

"Crazy old coot," Tammy murmured, shaking her head. She gave attention to the next customer in line, the sucker stick still poking down from her mouth. "Good mornin', what can I do for you today?"

Pen said nothing and dropped the duffle onto the floor. He motioned that he needed something to write on, queerly drawing circles in the air while mutely mouthing *write*.

"Is there somethin' wrong?" Tammy asked him, scrutinizing his face and trying to place a name to it. "You need somethin' to write on? Is that it?"

Pen nodded and smiled real friendly-like.

She handed him a blank deposit slip and an ink pen, and he began scrawling words on it. She glanced and shrugged bafflement to the woman teller working the next window.

After Pen finished writing, he slid the deposit slip back to her. Tammy warily picked up the paper and read it to herself.

"No. . . . I can't say that I do," she uttered, growing a bit alarmed. He remained mute, his face shining the goofy beam of an imbecile. He reached for another deposit slip and jotted more words. When he was done, he again gave it to her, and she read the words aloud this time.

"I used to wipe off ink stamp marks on these countertops and mop the floor you're standing on for ten dollars a day--"

"--But it was worth every damn dime for those cherry suckers you gave me," he ended the phrase.

Sudden recognition came to her clouded memory.

"My lands. . . Pen Cullen? Is that you?"

He grinned wide and flashed a wink. "Well, it sure ain't Jesse James."

"Gosh dawg. . . Lord knows it would be you pullin' a fast one on me like this." She patted her chest and breathed quick relief. "You had my poor ole heart racin' the dickens!"

●　●　●

For the next twenty minutes, he got an earful from Tammy Dixon. Tellings about her three grandsons and her seven great-grandkids. How the Almighty's hand had saved her from two heart surgeries. How her sixty-fifth birthday would come next May. How she was going to retire after working thirty-two years, and how she was going to celebrate her retirement party along with the bank's centennial commemoration. Then after she'd spouted all her soulful beliefs in how everything works out according to the Good Lord's mysterious ways, it dawned on her that Pen had come to straighten out the what-nots of his dead daddy's estate, so she shut her blabbering trap and escorted him to see the boss.

When they arrived at the open office door, Pen saw a bald and pudgy man sitting behind a mahogany desk and reading a bank pamphlet. He recognized him as Teddy Burns.

"Excuse me, Mr. Burns?" Tammy announced.

The nerdy banker turned his head up.

"You remember Pen Cullen?"

Burns gave a look of surprise and placed his reading material down on the desk. "Well, sure. Sure, I know Pen Cullen."

Pen stepped inside and nodded with a grin. "Good to see you, Teddy."

"I go by Ted now." Burns nodded back and offered his hand and when Pen felt the bank man's spongy palm, he remembered what a sissy boy Burns had been back in their school days. Kids used to call him Butt Burns.

"Alright then, Ted." He said it mockingly. "You always were good in Math, now here you are runnin' the damn bank."

"Yeah, yeah, in the blood you might say," Burns agreed, humbly. "But I'm only holdin' down the fort until Mr. Hobson recovers from his illness."

"Oh yeah? What's he got?"

"Not real sure. He don't like to tell too much, you know how he is. Too much pride in him."

"Yeah, that sounds like him alright."

Tammy raised her hand and interrupted. "Well, I'll let you men get to your business, but Pen I wanna hear what all you're up to these days."

"Oh, you know me, Tammy. Up to no good."

"I wouldn't doubt it." Her eyes teasingly rolled.

Burns raised his finger to draw her attention. "Hey Tammy, can you, uhm, tell Susie to get Frank Carter on the phone for me?"

"Yes sir, I sure will."

After Tammy stepped out, Burns pulled a chair away from the front side of his desk and gestured gentlemanly with his spongy hand. "Here you go, Pen, have yourself a seat."

Pen set his duffle onto the floor and leisurely plopped down into the chair. It felt like he'd fallen onto a cloud. His head was spinning from the lack of sleep and the anxiousness of finally making it to the moment of why he'd come back to Doe Run.

"Whew, I sure wasn't expectin' to see you pop in this mornin," Burns said, forging a banker's grin. "One of our lawyers must've spent four or five months diggin' up some sort of address for you, and I think he come up with six or seven different ones."

"Yeah, I ain't found the right place to settle down just yet," Pen answered in a playful tone, casually finding his pack of Camels in his shirt pocket. "But from your letter I figured I better come real quick. Okay if I smoke in here?"

"Oh sure. Sure." Burns opened a desk drawer and took out a glass ashtray with the bank's name on it. He slid it across the mahogany desktop.

"Thanks." Pen flamed up a cigarette. "Glad to see some things ain't changed much here. Gettin' to be a man can't even light up inside anymore." His sight peered up at two mounted deer heads on the wall, then his eyes turned to peer out through the glass walls. "Bank pretty much looks the same."

"Well, there's a few new whatnots, we've not stayed entirely backwoods," Burns replied, with a joking wink. "We bought us a fancy computer to run the check processor not too long back, and I ordered one of those teller machines the other day. The kind where you stick a card in it, and it spits your money out."

"Oh sure, I seen them before."

"They had one at a bank over in Springfield, and the second I saw it, I knew we just had to get us one." Burns leaned over the desk to whisper. "Except now all the gals out there's got their panties in a wad, believin' they're gonna get replaced by robots."

"Gettin' big city, are you?"

"Now I wouldn't go that far," Burns replied, waving his sweaty hand like he was swatting a fly. "We still say yes sir and yes ma'am."

"Well, that's good to hear," Pen said, with the tone of his voice falling back into its natural-born Missouri twang. "Hell, I still miss the easy way of life here. Sometimes I even go to wishin' I was the janitor of this here bank again."

"Janitor?" Burns cocked his head.

"Back in high school," Pen affirmed. "Used to clean up in the late afternoons. Mostly just dumped the trash and mopped."

"Huh," Burns huffed. "Guess I never knew that."

"Well, we didn't really talk much back then Teddy."

"No, I reckon not," Burns said with a hint of remembered embarrassment. "But I remember you well enough. Shoot, we only had a graduating class of fifty-two."

Pen blew a puff of smoke across the table. "I also did a short turn as a repo man for Mr. Hobson," he said, remembering it just now. "Found out real quick that folks don't like lettin' go of their stuff, even if they don't pay for it."

"I'm afraid that hasn't changed much. We hire a big outfit out of Rolla to handle our repositions now, and they're worth every penny."

Pen again looked out into the lobby, his mind filling with memories he'd forgotten. "I remember one time I had to go get a truck from one of those backwoods families livin' out in Buxton Holler. Over there near Owl's Bend?"

"Oh sure, I've been out that way fishin' before."

"This old boy had bought himself a Ford pickup and hadn't paid one red cent on the loan for goin' on like eight or nine months. Forget his name. Anyhow, Mr. Hobson was pissed as all hell that he'd loaned money to him, and he promised to pay me two hundred dollars if I went and brung that new truck back to town. Well hell, two hundred bucks was a hell of a lot back then."

"So you went and got it?"

"I did. Wasn't easy though. You grew up hearin' those same stories about them cross-eyed hillbillies shootin' anyone comin' on their land."

"Oh yes. Goin' back for years."

Pen tapped his cigarette and leaned back in the chair and his voice dropped into a more dramatic spirit in the telling of the tale.

"Well I got Byron Tisdale to back me up and we drove out to Buxton Holler, we like to never find where the guy lived back in those hills. Took us probably three, four hours. But when we finally got there, there sat that new Ford pickup. I told Byron to wait in my truck while I snuck up the driveway to see if I could hotwire it, and hell if six, seven hounds came barkin' from around the house. It's a goddamn wonder I didn't get my leg ate off."

Pen sucked a long drag and let the smoke curl out from the corner of his mouth. Burns sat stone still with anticipation.

"Well about the time I got underneath the dash and workin' the wires, this bareass naked girl came barrelin' out the house. She starts screamin' and carryin' on, then out comes this sum bitch behind her, just as bareass as she is."

Burns' goofy face etched in a clownish grin. "You mean neither of them had no clothes on?"

"Naked as jailbirds. Big ole titties floppin' over her belly, and his prick standin' up like a goddamn light pole."

"Good Lord."

"Well, I rolled up the window right quick, and locked the damn doors, and it's all I could do to hotwire that goddamn Ford before the crazy fucker came at me. I threw it in gear and took off, but hell if he didn't hop in back of the damn truckbed."

Pen grinned and took a drag and flicked his ash.

"Man, I floored it and went flyin' down that log road, hittin' every chug hole and sailin' in the air, and it must've been a whole mile before I threw him out of the bed on his bare ass."

"Ogghh shoot, that must've hurt."

"Yeah. I's scared I might've killed the fucker, so I shoved it in reverse to make sure he was alright, and hell if he didn't jump up on one leg and start comin' at me again. All I could do was laugh. I yelled out to him that I was sorry about interruptin' him and his lady. Then I drove on and left the dipshit standin' there holdin' his hard dick in his hand."

"You mean, it never went down?"

Pen winked. "Guess I should've asked what kind of water he's drinkin' out there in those woods. Might've had me a sip."

Burns busted out with hearty laughter.

Pen smiled and tapped his cigarette. He gazed out into the lobby again, amused by his wild self of yesteryear. "I about forgot all the crazy shit I used to do when I was younger."

"Oh boy, whew," Burns exhaled his laughter, trying to rein it in. "That was a good one, alright. A real good one." He cleared his throat and began wiping his sweaty brow with a kerchief. "The gals are gonna go to thinkin' I've took up liquor in the mornin', hearin' me bawlin' in here like this."

"Got a bottle in one of those desk drawers?"

"No, no, no, now. Don't you go tempting me."

"You're the boss man, ain't you?"

Burn raised his hand in surrender and coughed down his last giggles and turned serious to the matter at hand.

"Well, I sure wish I would've known you were comin' by this mornin'. I would've had the papers drawn up."

Pen shrugged. "Aww, I'm not particular on papers. We can just cut the check and call it a good day."

"Oh. . ." Burns beamed a short sigh of relief. "So you're definitely wantin' to take over the payments then?"

"Payments hell, I'm not askin' for no loan." Pen smirked at the banker's bad stab of humor. "How much is it all worth?"

"Well, thankfully, the house and property still cover most of what he owed. Course, the tornado that hit last spring put a hurtin' on the overall value."

Pen squinted puzzlement. "What he owed?"

"On the loans," Burns replied, nodding like it was common knowledge. "That's why you're here, right?"

"I don't know shit about no loans," Pen huffed. "I just come to settle up with however much money there is from the estate."

"You, don't know about the loans?" Burns raised his eyebrows, a bit flabbergasted. "My letter explained it all."

"I said I got your letter," Pen replied, his voice deepening with irritation. "I didn't say I read it all."

The banker's grin dropped into a banker's frown. "Well, uhm, truth is, I sent that letter to let you know that the house was foreclosed on and was up for sale."

Pen leaned forward and tapped his ash and glared at Burns.

"Teddy, I appreciate your niceties, but can we cut to the nut? I haven't known if my dad was alive for thirteen years, and sure didn't know he was finally dead till your goddamn letter came. So what the fuck are you tryin' to say?"

Burns gulped and steeled his nerves in attempt to explain.

"Well, see, your dad, uhm, he had taken out a second mortgage with us about five years ago. And then, he went ahead and took out a couple more smaller loans by using his savings here as collateral. And well, he never paid a dime to us. And I thought maybe you might want to buy the house back at cost since it was your home and all. It was all in the letter."

Pen glared at the sissy banker, fighting a strong urge to reach across the desk and throttle his larynx.

"How much?"

"How much what?"

"How much were the fuckin' loans?"

"Around eighty thousand. All together. I tried to work out an arrangement with him, but he never seemed to care much about listenin' to me. Then after the tornado hit, I found out from the insurance company that he wasn't keepin' regular payment on the home insurance neither."

"Tornado?"

"The one that hit last spring," Burns told him like he should already know. "It was the strangest thing. Only touched down in a couple parts of town then shot back up in the sky like it had been aimin' or somethin'." Burns frowned. "It did hit your house, I'm afraid. Not as bad as most of the others around it, but enough damage to lower the worth about twenty-five thousand."

Pen stabbed the Camel butt into the ashtray and let the bad news take full hold.

"Nobody here at the bank asked what your dad was wantin' his loans for. It's not our usual place to ask such things so long as a customer's collateral is good. But I'm guessin' now that he was usin' the borrowed money to live off of, cause he didn't have no income as far as I could find out."

Pen blew out a strained breath.

"So there's nothin'?"

Burns tightened his mouth with sorrow. "Like I said, I tried a bunch of times to talk to him about how to repay the money. But he never came to the door or answered my phone calls."

"And the only reason you sent your letter to me was to see if I wanted to buy the place back?"

The chunky secretary with the big hairdo appeared at the open door. "Mr. Burns, Frank Carter is on line one."

"Thank you, Susie," replied Burns, exhaling relief for the break in tension. "Excuse me, Pen, this is about your dad's bank records." He picked up his phone and punched the line one button. "Hello Frank. How are you? Yes sir. Yes sir,

Pen Cullen is right here in my office. Yes sir, that's right, the Cullen estate."

As Burns droned on the phone, Pen lit up another cigarette, sucking the smoke hard into his lungs, trying to curtail the outrage rising in his chest. He glared at one of the mounted deer heads on the wall and imagined himself ripping it down and smashing it on the mahogany desk.

"Oh, I see," Burns went on with his phone call. "No, I understand. Sure. Sure. Tell you what Frank, let me ask him and see what I can work out and I'll give you a call back in a few minutes. Will do. Thanks now."

Burns hung up the phone and exhaled.

"That was the bank's attorney, Frank Carter, he's in charge of the bank's legal work. He's also the one who found your addresses."

Pen kept looking at the mounted deer heads, saying nothing in return.

"How long you plannin' on being in town?"

"I wasn't plannin' on it."

"Well Frank lives over in Poplar Bluff, but he said he can make it here with the records and whatnot Friday mornin'."

"Records of what? How broke he was?"

Burns pursed his lips, catching the blister in Pen's response. "I'm real sorry about this mix-up, Pen. I sure didn't mean for you to come all this way to find out like this. Shoot, I liked your dad. It's still sort of a shock to me that he's passed away. I was the one who talked the bank owners into lettin' him stay in the house after the tornado hit."

Pen peeled eyes away from the deer heads and stared his hatred at Burns. "Don't feel too bad for him, Teddy. I used to watch the rotten son of bitch charm the rattle off a diamondhead right before he cut its fuckin' head off."

9

PEN'S WALK FROM THE TOWN & COUNTY BANK back to Jessup's gas station was a dour and sour one. His daddy's worthlessness was not at all what he'd come back home to get, and he was now hating him more than ever, even if the sideways prick was six feet down in the dirt.

As soon as he arrived at the station, yellow-teeth Wayne gave him the word that Junior had already towed in the Firebird. The black beauty appeared to be fine, save for the few dents and scratches. Still, the two goofy greaseheads kindly asked if they could check out the motor, change the oil, kick the tires, as it wasn't every day that they got to inspect such a sweet beast. And since it was for no charge, Pen obliged them.

He waited on the bench that old Jim Jessup used to sit on, and after a short while, he reclined for a hopeful catnap. But the speed and black coffee kept his thoughts whirling wild, bouncing between what was past and what was now, and measuring if there was any difference. Thirteen years had gone by since he'd promised himself that he would never come back to Doe Run, and yet here he was. Still pissed-off. Still broke. Still desperate. Then his lingering thoughts drifted back to his formative days with Tara Hawkins.

It was at the start of fifth grade when she'd moved to Doe Run from Pigott, Arkansas. Her folks were the newly hired elementary school teachers, and so right off, all the kids either brown-nosed her for favors or figured she was a snotty snitch. He himself didn't carry much opinion for her. She was little more than a scrawny girl who wore fancy dresses and thick wire-rimmed glasses, and he paid her little mind during his boyhood trials of riding dirt bikes and skipping flat rocks across ponds and shooting BB guns and sling slots with his good buddy Byron.

However, as the seasons came and went, nature altered the halcyon lives of the boys. Muscles ripped harder, voices sank deeper, and dark hairs sprouted on milky skin. It was during this strange metamorphosis that Tara Hawkins bravely stepped up to him at the Junior High dance and dared him for a boogie down on the gym floor. Under the rainbow strobe lights, he noticed her dorky spectacles were absent from her face and her stringy hair had dropped in drooping curls. He thought she was pretty enough, but he wasn't fond of her boney body, which could barely hang up her white dress. Neither did he like the metal braces on her teeth. His harshest judgment fell upon the puny buds on her chest, which equaled the size of strawberries. But as she stood there waiting for his fateful decision to join her or not, his pubescent mind began to speculate the odds of whether she might be desperate enough to let him French kiss her. So with no lost dignity in trying, he yanked himself up off the bleachers and they began dancing.

Once the slow songs had ended and all the waltzing

couples were told by the teachers to break apart and go home, they walked outside hand-in-hand, not wanting to part. In a whispery voice he asked if she wished to sneak away to the shadows before her parents saw them together. She beamed bashful delight, and they hurried off to a dark narrow space between the gym and cafeteria, and there their writhing bodies bonded and their wet tongues wrestled.

After the star-crossed night at the Junior High dance, he did not utter more than ten words to her again till the summer they both turned sixteen. He was wheeling through the side streets of town in a junk '66 Chevy truck that he had bargained for $300 from a penniless farmer, and as he cruised through the park, he came upon her lying on a beach towel in the hot dry grass. She was wearing red short-shorts and a pink halter top, and the rest of her was bare oiled skin soaking up the bright sun's rays. He eased on the gas and gawked at her slim tan legs and her slim tan arms and her coffee-brown hair that ran down her smooth back, and he noticed how her strawberry buds had ripened to plump peaches. Right then and there he knew that Tara Hawkins was the prettiest girl he had ever seen. And by the time high school started again in late-August, his charming ways and charming words had already stolen her heart.

Because Tara's folks were Christian, and wary of boys with rowdy repute, they only allowed her to tutor him in their school studies from time to time. Between sneaking quick kisses, she taught him geometry and algebraic equations, and the Mississippi River tale of Huck and Jim, and of all the civilities and wars of mankind. And as the pleasurable afternoons of nurturing his wisdom wore on and on, her burning female urges kept rising to take flame, and so on Christmas Eve, a little before midnight, they snuck away together and drove out to a snowy backroad, and there she gifted him her virginity on the cramped cold seat of his '66 Chevy.

Once the deed was done between them, nothing could douse the heat in their hearts and the lust in their loins. To avoid her watchful folks, they sometimes skipped school in the middle of the day to slip off to the countryside where they would share their young bodies and share their young minds. He told her how much he missed his dead mother, and how much he hated his cruel father, and how he sometimes wished he had been born as someone else at some other place at some other time. In turn, she would listen to all his sorrows and share in all his dreams, and together they softly spoke of all the tomorrows and tomorrows they would spend with one another.

Upon their graduation from school in the spring, the young lovers began their furtive plan of elopement to Memphis in the fall. All that was needed was to keep their secret from her folks and to save enough cash to get out of Doe Run. Tara took on as a waitress at the Queenway Diner while he procured a hellish job at a local sawmill with Byron. Wages for cutting timber were decent for strong young men, yet he spent most of his working days grumbling about the burdensome toils of hard labor and pining for a better future. More than a few times he declared to Byron that he was never going to become like his rotten daddy, the type of bastard who cheated and lied till he hated every damn thing in the world. He also swore that whatever happened in his destined life, he'd be happy so long as Tara was there.

"Good news, bud."

Pen's eyes popped open and his memories of Tara Hawkins morphed into the face of yellow-teeth Wayne grinning down at him.

"No major damage done."

Pen inhaled a lengthy breath to clear his muddled mind, and he rose from Jim Jessup's bench like he was crawling out of a grave. "A car like that, a dent is major damage," he reminded Wayne.

"Yessir, you sure got yourself quite a classic there."

Pen stretched his body and patted his jacket for his Camels, his fogged mind still trying to deduce what was dream and what was real, what was past and what was now. He found his cigarettes and lit one.

"I hear you say you's from around here?"

"Not in a long while."

"I moved here from over in Piedmont, about eight, nine years ago. My wife's from here though. Cheri Abrams, you know her?"

"Her dad haul propane?"

"Yeah, yeah, that's her alright. She's a pretty good ole gal. Pretty good for me anyways."

Pen smiled to himself, remembering the gossip of how Cheri Abrams had once spread her legs for three different boys in one night on a Future Farmers of America's hayride.

"We got'cha gas filled up like you asked," Wayne announced, blowing a wad of snot into his greasy rag. "I reckon I can give you a local rate on the tow."

"How much is that?"

"How about we just call it fifty square?"

Pen reached for his wallet from his hind pocket. "Shit," he grumbled once he opened it. "Didn't realize I was runnin' so short."

"We take credit cards."

"Had to give them up." Pen grimaced, stalling. "You mind if I come back and catch you later?"

Wayne pinched his face and scratched his whiskers with his greasy fingers. "Well, we don't normally do that."

"You can call up Tammy Dixon over at the bank." Pen voiced his words with good old boy confidence. "She knows I'm good for it. I just gotta get some paperwork done on my family estate and all, you know how fuckin' banks are."

Wayne considered the dilemma as if it held a life-or-death decision. He pulled his greasy cap off his greasy head and ran his greasy palm over his greasy hair. "Well, I guess if you ain't got the dough, you ain't got the dough. You say you'll bring it soon?"

"Cross my heart, hope to die," Pen swore and winked. He stuck his wallet back into his pocket. "Nice to be back in a town that's still neighborly."

10

HE HAD FIBBED TO YELLOW-TEETH WAYNE. He knew that there was plenty enough cash stuck inside his boot to take care of the tow and gas. But since this odyssey back home had become such a chain of unforeseen disasters, he also knew that he needed to splurge his dwindling funds on some strong liquor to kill his growing angst before he did something foolish and desperate.

After steering the Firebird out of Jessup's gas station, he made a beeline for Yonker's liquor store. He bought a fifth of Wild Turkey and a case of cold Budweiser while listening to old Ray Yonker carp complaints about the state of the world. He then headed in the direction of Joe Silva's farm, as his old Mexican mentor was the only person in town he cared to see. And hell, if Byron Tisdale happened to be there, he reckoned they could maybe rekindle some good time memories together, too.

He traveled eastward on Highway 21, a road as curvy and treacherous as the devil's rollercoaster to hell. It seemed every mile marked a small shrine or cross stuck in the dirt beside the ditch where some poor sucker had met death by wreck. Dead drunks. Dead truckers. Dead hotrod teens. The most profound one was the double cross where twin brothers had met in different cars in opposite lanes and had played a game of chicken, only to meet head-on and die together in a crash of speeding metal.

After fifteen rolling miles of two-lane curves and jumpy hills, he finally came to a black mailbox with the name Jose Silva painted cursively in white. He slowed and turned onto a gravel crossroad that curled and vanished back into a curtain of woods, and a hundred yards down the gravel he spotted a *no trespassing* sign nailed onto a tree.

The way Joe told it, back in the mid-60s he was browsing a Texas newspaper and came across a back-page ad for cheap acreage for sale in southern Missouri, and something in his soul stirred and told him to buy it. He purchased the hundred-and-sixty acres sight unseen, using the money he had saved from his six years in the Navy. Then as soon as he arrived at his new midsouth homeland, he got the bright idea to plant a crop of beans. He arranged a hush-hush deal with a logging outfit to strip eighty acres of timber, and then he plowed the empty space. Problem was, none of the locals explained to him that the solid mountain ground he had bought was only good for growing rocks and briars, and after the first two harvesting seasons, he caught on that he'd been had.

Even though he struck out with farming, Joe remained determined to stay in the Ozarks. He built himself a one-story cabin made entirely of concrete cinder blocks and timber beams. Once the modest homestead was square enough to live in, he set up a welding shop in town to earn his keep. At first folks didn't know what to make of a Mexican, him being the sole brownskin in a hundred-mile radius. Generally, they didn't trust any foreigners, and none of them gave a good goddamn that Joe was a U.S. citizen born in Texas. Still, he graciously accepted his secondary role instead of getting all civil rights on the racist hillbillies. He figured the half-wits might eventually come around to trusting him easier that way, and thus make his welding business more profitable. And sure enough, his notion proved right. After a handful of years, he became sort of the town mascot. Then he drove up his prices on the white sons of bitches.

Pen didn't come to know Joe until his freshman year in high school when he and Byron were told by the basketball coach that they possessed rebellious attitudes, and their troublesome kind were not welcome to join the team. So rather than play roundball like the other energetic high school boys, they were forced to find part-time jobs to keep themselves out of serious troubles. Since Pen's dead mom had once worked at the Town & County Bank, the bank's president, Mr. Hobson, held sympathy for her only son, so for the grand prize of $3.15 an hour he got to perform the thankless duties of sweeping floors, polishing countertops, wiping windows, and scrubbing piss-tainted stools. Meanwhile, Byron found a much cooler job at Joe's welding shop because the Mexican liked that the stout spooky kid was strong as an ox and didn't jabber much.

The boys soon discovered that Joe Silva was the only man who could honestly identify with their complexities of teenage boy belligerence. Joe told them that he had carried plenty of it himself before he had liberated his anger in the Navy, and he invited them to come out to his farm whenever they felt the need to let off some steam. He gave them dips of snuff, let them smoke sweet cigars, and once in a while he let them get hammered on rotgut mescal and homemade wine. Other times they would tree coons with stray hounds, or gig bullfrogs at midnight in the ponds, and every now and again Joe would break out his matching pair of Smith & Wesson .44 Magnum six-shooters he had brought with him from his boyhood days in El Paso. In many ways, Joe filled the consequential role of a loving father to them much better than their no-account daddies.

The Firebird bounced and nearly bottomed out in a deep gully, its underside scraping against rock and mud.

"Holy fuck!" Pen yelled at the gravel path in front of him, which was at least two winters past from a grading.

After a couple more miles of bouncing and crawling over dried-up mud holes and washes, and passing seven more no trespassing signs, the Firebird came to the top of a high hill slope that stood above a valley of rocky farmland. As Pen braked down the other side, he could just glimpse the shoddy one-story cabin and the rusted tin roof of the weathered-gray barn standing behind it. When he hit the bottom of the hill he looked off to the rocky barren pasture and to his left he saw the bony shapes of six horses and a lone jackass. They looked to be a couple of paint mares, an appaloosa gelding, and the rest were Shetland ponies. All of them, including the old jack, gave the appearance of wild.

He drove on and went past the useless machinery that Joe had taken in trade over the years for his various welding jobs. There sat a Case hay baler and a four-spiral rake, neither of which had been in a field for a decade, and next to them a '56 Farmall tractor with a rusted bush hog hitched on the ball, and a weathered wagon with four flat tires.

As he got closer to the cabin, he noticed its cinder block foundation and walls still didn't have a drop of paint slapped on, and he recalled that Joe never quite finished anything he started. His eyes then looked up to the rooftop and saw the fighting cock weathervane pointing south, and a trail of smoke was rising from the rock chimney.

Figuring someone must be home, he pulled the Firebird behind the rusted Dodge Ram parked in the driveway, and as he killed the engine, a huge man barreled out the front door, violently gesticulating a fire poker in his hand, and screaming something about trespassing signs.

Pen gingerly hopped out of the Firebird, holding up his hands in surrender. The angry man was wearing a pair of stained long john bottoms, his top half was naked and white as a catfish's belly, and the black hair grown over his square head and pudgy face was tangled like a patch of briars. Still, there was no mistaking those crystal gray eyes. Even as bloodshot as they were.

"Damn man." Pen grinned. "You sure growed up to be an ugly mother fucker."

Byron was so soused on Ten High that his vision couldn't quite make out the visitor's facial features, yet he could vaguely recognize the voice.

"Pen?"

"Who'd you think I was? Santa Claus?"

Byron drunkenly gazed down the gravel road as though expecting Custer's cavalry to come charging down the steep hill. When nothing appeared, he gradually relaxed the poker down to his side. "Caught me nappin'," he slurred, shaking the chaos out of his skull.

"Well wake the hell up." Pen bent down inside the Firebird and hoisted out the bottle of Wild Turkey. "I was figurin' on doin' some drinkin' with you and Joe. Where is the damn old greaser?"

"El Paso."

"El Paso?" Pen scoffed. "Shit. Really?"

Byron rubbed his forehead, his dull judgment still stuck in the fumes of the liquor he'd drunk for breakfast.

"How'd you know I's here?"

Pen hesitated, weighing the answer.

"Your wife told me."

They then both got real quiet and stared at one another like they had both sunk into a shared dream. Except it wasn't a dream, it was the thirteen years that had passed them by and the queer wonderment if they could still consider themselves as friends.

11

STANDING AT THE KITCHEN COUNTER, Pen poured Wild Turkey into a couple of jelly-jar glasses. His nose caught a strong whiff of a rank odor polluting the room and he figured it must be the stack of food-coated plates and crusted pots in the sink. Or maybe the empty soup cans and soiled paper towels scattered across the filthy concrete floor. He guessed a tidy woman had not graced the place for a long spell.

Byron stumbled into the kitchen from the back bedroom, sipping a Budweiser bottle. He had tossed on a holey t-shirt and a pair of grimy jeans to look more decent for company.

"Well look at you, Pretty Boy Floyd."

Pen crossed the floor and handed over one of the jelly-jars of Wild Turkey. They tapped the glass jars and tipped them to their lips and let the strong brown liquid slide down their throats.

"Goddamn," Pen declared. "That there's the answer I've been lookin' for."

Byron showed no reaction.

"So when's Joe's gettin' back from El Paso?"

"Sometime in spring."

"He go there to get himself some Mexican clam over the border?"

"Only said he needed to get to the desert for his joints."

"Shit," Pen snickered. "He must be gettin' old then."

Byron left the conversation there by wandering toward the kitchen table. He picked up a sticky jar of syrupy goo sitting next to a plate of fried meat and unscrewed the cap.

"What'cha got there?"

"Sorghum."

"No, the meat."

"Dove."

"Dove?" Pen scoffed. "You got somethin' against frozen pizza?"

Byron poured sorghum over the soft bird breast. "There's a hunk of braunschweiger in the fridge if you want it."

The mention of liver paste sounded even more disgusting to Pen. So he walked over and reached for the plate of bird and worked a small bite of it into his jaw.

"Little tough."

Byron again didn't acknowledge Pen's verbal jabs at gabbing over things of no importance and he reclined into a chair at the table. Pen followed suit. They took more sips of whiskey. And gawked at one another with a mixture of amazement and suspicion.

"Heard your dad died," Byron mumbled.

"Please. Don't be bringin' that fucker up."

"Take it you ain't broke up over it?"

"Just put the final piece of the puzzle in place is all."

Byron swallowed a bite of meat with a wash of bourbon, his crystal eyes leveling toward his guest.

"What'd she say about me?"

"What?"

"My ex-bitch. What'd she say about me?"

Pen stared at the bourbon in his glass and swished it.

"Just that you's stayin' out here."

"She preach that Jesus shit at you?"

"She didn't say a whole hell of a lot to tell you the truth." Pen told his words carefully. "I just stopped at the Queenway for some breakfast and saw her still workin' there."

"She can keep all that fairytale bullshit she wants to herself. I ain't havin' none of it."

Pen squinted in question.

"You sayin' she's a born-again?"

"Up there at that Church of Christ." Byron sniffed. "She moved in with the goddamn preacher."

"You're shittin'."

"Goin' on six, seven months."

Pen waited for the punchline, one side of his mouth curling up. "That how you come to be stayin' out here?"

"Joe just asked me to keep an eye on the place while he's gone. I'm livin' back home with my dad."

Pen stayed hushed for another moment, disbelieving that Tara was a born-again gal living in sin with a holy man. He suddenly didn't want to talk about her anymore.

"Your dad still layin' blacktop for the state?"

"Yeah. He ain't got much else to do with mom gone."

"Where'd she go?"

"Offed herself on pills."

Pen rolled his tongue in his mouth before responding to the morbid news. "How long ago?"

"Five years. Come Christmas."

"Christmas Day?"

Byron raised in glass in a toast.

"Her last present."

Pen stared at the grown-up version of the fat kid he once knew. What he saw was a stranger who was drunk and smelly and bizarre. He pulled a pack of smokes from his shirt pocket and tapped one out and then another.

"Want a smoke?"

He slid the extra Camel across the table. He lit his then stretched across the table with his Zippo to share the flame.

"Where you workin' these days?"

"Lookin' at it," Byron grunted, smoke flaring down his nostrils. "I's deputy game warden for a while."

"Deputy game warden?" Pen chuckled. "They give you a badge?"

"Naw. Ain't even such a thing as deputy game warden. Had to say deputy cause I ain't got no college. Like it'd make a shit of difference."

"How you gettin' by then?"

"Government check." Byron queerly stared at the lit end of his cigarette. "Guess you didn't go become one those movie star fags like you used to say you's gonna do."

"Christ," Pen snorted. "Not hardly. Cleaned the pools of some of 'em though."

"Movie stars or fags?"

"Ain't no difference really."

They quieted. Smoke clouds hovering between them. Byron pushed his spent Camel into an empty Bud bottle. Then he rose from his chair as if he wished to escape and drunkenly keeled over onto the table.

"Whoa, whoa there, hoss," Pen reacted.

Byron stood back erect and swayed in his boots.

"You alright there, man?"

"Gotta feed the horses," Byron answered. Then he staggered out of the kitchen without another word.

"Well, do you need some help?" Pen yelled out.

No answer returned.

"Hey By? You need any help? By?"

Again, nothing.

Pen blew smoke from his puckered lips. He marveled over how the fat kid with the crystal gray eyes had become even more odd as a full-grown man. And he tried to not remember how much he had hated the crazy bastard for stealing Tara away from him.

12

THE HISS OF BURNING COALS were sizzling in his ears and caused him to jolt awake.

An orange hue illuminated the room.

His hazy vision set upon an Aztec death mask glaring down at him from the wall. Its demonic face had pearl shell and turquoise embedded around its empty eye sockets, and its gaping mouth gave the stark impression that it was a man-eating god.

Joe's, he remembered. *I'm at Joe's.*

He inhaled a breath of smoky air and rubbed his sleepy eyes with the heel of his hand. His tongue felt like a piece of concrete inside his parched mouth and his throat burned dry when he tried to swallow. He glanced at the clock on the mantle and it told him it was 1:17 AM.

He tossed the scratchy Mexican blanket off his body and sat up on the edge of the couch and glanced at the relics in the room. The bleached-white skull of a Texas longhorn and the faded poster that bore the name of a matador named Carlos Arruza appearing in Juarez. On the opposite wall was a coyote skin stretched out next to the hung antlers of a ten-point buck, and on the mantle lay a stone battle-ax and feathered kachina doll, along with a bevy of crooked arrowhead shards and a silver pair of cowboy spurs.

He rose from the couch and lumbered to the window and pulled back the red muslin curtains. Dampness fogged the glass. He wiped it off with his fingers, but he still saw nothing outside besides a starless sky of blackness.

He backed away from the foggy window and headed into the kitchen. On the table sat the empty bottle of 101-proof, next to the plate of dove bones and a dozen empty Budweiser bottles. He guessed that after he'd dozed off on the couch, Byron must've had himself a hell of a party.

He idled his way to the sink and turned on the faucet. He grabbed a dirty jelly-jar glass off the counter, rinsed it out with a few needed sloshes, then filled it to the rim with cold water. As he brought the glass to his bone-dry mouth, his ears perked at an ill-omen noise that sounded like the boogeyman hovering over his shoulder.

Probably the wind, he told himself.

When he shut off the tap, the eerie noise came again.

His curiosity took hold. He soft-stepped out of the kitchen and entered the short hallway that led back to the bedroom. It was pitch dark, so he took the Zippo from his jeans pocket and flicked it on. He tiptoed down the dark narrow hall, and when he came to the bedroom door, he squeezed his fingers through the crack to open it wider. With the faint illumination of the Zippo's flame, he could see Byron flat on his back in bed, madly moaning and trembling something fierce.

He shut down the lighter and closed the door. Then he backtracked down the unlit hallway and went into the living room. He bent to the sizzling coals in the fireplace and tried to prod them to flame with the poker. The spitting sparks declined to rise from the ashes, so he lifted out a fresh log from the woodbox near the hearth and tossed it in.

Once the fire was going again, he shuffled over to his duffle lying at the head of the couch. His hand rummaged through it and brought out a tablet of writing paper and a lead pencil. His hand went inside a second time and pulled out a sandwich bag stuffed with sticky dope buds and a pack of Zig Zag papers.

With his handful of items, he plopped down on the calf-skin chair and went to work on rolling a finger-size joint. By the time he lit it with the Zippo, the flames in the fireplace were licking high and happy across the fresh log.

While the dope smoke held in his lungs, he opened the writing tablet onto his lap. As a young boy, he had possessed the gift of drawing whatever his mind could see in memory, but with age he had lost most of the talent. As a man, he could only sketch vague depictions of certain images burned deep into his brain, so the face he began to scrawl upon the page was not the face of the frail woman he had seen at the Queenway today, but rather the face of the young girl his heart had once fondly known.

TWO DAYS UNTIL
DEER SEASON

13

AS HAD BEEN HIS EVERYDAY ROUTINE, Byron had stumbled out of bed before dawn, and under the blanket of darkness, he had headed to the ancient woods of Osage Bend. It didn't matter a lick that his old buddy Pen Cullen had dropped in out of the blue.

He took his usual route of three county highways and then he turned off on the rutted log road. Five miles deep into the heart of the woods, he parked the Ram at his spot where the rutted path ended. The only alteration he would make today is that he would leave the unsealed fifth of Ten High under the seat because he didn't want to risk puking again. Draining that bottle of 101 last night would just have to tide him over for a spell.

It took him till near sunrise to trek the two-mile stretch to the blind. When he arrived at the salt block and worn-out tire, he saw that someone else had been there and had scattered corn kernels on the ground.

Stupid sack of shit was his first thought. Even an ignorant jackass would be smart enough to know that the monster buck had gotten to be a monster by being extra cautious, and it could get plenty spooked by a mere whiff of fresh bait placed at an already established hunt site.

As he stood staring crossly at the yellow kernels, the taunting laughs from a trio of crows cackled from above. Gazing upward, he staunchly reminded himself that they were only fiendish fowl, not the evil haints that haunted his daily dreams. Even so, he wished he had a shotgun so he could blow their laughing asses right out of the goddamn sky.

After the black birds had flown from his sight, he traveled onward. He soon came to the black oak and the blind. And he found fresh boot prints packed into the dirt.

He hunched down and scrutinized them as if they belonged to a mysterious beast, though he already suspected they belonged to the sack of shit who'd spread the corn. The sack of shit must've come out late yesterday afternoon, long after he himself had gone, and the sack of shit must've also climbed up to the blind for a look-see.

He stood back up and studied the black oak's branches. His weakened will was reluctant to make the climb, until his dogged nature told his jitters that they'd just have to shut up and swallow their pride today.

After he'd laddered up the trunk and heaved himself upon the creaky boards, he felt the familiar wave of black bile sweep through his tightened belly. So rather than standing high in his exalted tree throne, he thought it best to stay on his haunches. And there, he watched and listened to another morning in Osage Bend spring alive.

He knew these woods well. He had been coming here since the spring winds first whistled through the green leaves. When the purple milkweed and the rose verbena had painted the dark ground. When the blossoms of redbud and buckthorn had graced the hills. When yellow-throated warblers and white-eyed vireos had fluttered their romances between the thickets. Many times his bearded face had breached the weaved webs of yellow-spotted spiders. Many times his lumbering legs had strode over the coils of copperheads. One time he had watched a black serpent, swum in from the rising rivers, stretch its cottonmouth to strike and swallow a hare whole. Another time he had awakened upon the ferns to behold the monster buck in its summer velvet, escorting its harem of does and bloodline of suckling fawns. Often he had dined on morels and chicory flowers, had drunk the sugary juice of berries. Had pulled legions of ticks and chiggers from his itching skin, had twice caught poison ivy, and had spent whole days watching armies of blue dragons and orange butterflies share their wings with floating seeds.

But now it was late fall. The rising sun was concealed behind dreary clouds. He could only see a few scurrying gray squirrels and a lone red-cockaded woodpecker. Could only hear the distant gobble of a tom turkey. Still, these ancient woods remained his only refuge. The place where he could hide his fear from the haints. The place where he allowed himself to remember when his little boy was still alive.

And so, as the melodic rain began dancing between the branches, he stayed upon his high wilderness throne and dreamed of when his life was not so broken.

14

AT AROUND NINE O'CLOCK in the morning Pen roused on the couch, this time remembering where he was. He tossed the scratchy Mexican blanket off his aching body and sat up to rub the green slime out from his eyes. After he shook the cobwebs from his sluggish noggin, he stood and drowsily staggered for the toilet down the hallway. He relieved himself and splashed his sleepy face awake with cold water, then shuffled out of the bathroom to notice the bedroom door was open half-way.

"Hey By, you up?"

When no answer came, he peeped in and saw the bed unmade and empty. "Crazy fuck," he groaned, hacking up cigarette tar from his lungs.

He sauntered back down the hallway and through the kitchen and went to the front door and opened it. He saw the Ram was not there, so he closed the door and headed back into the living room. He looked around, trying to think of something important to do, and his eyes came to the Zenith television propped up on milk crates in the corner.

He shuffled to it and pulled the dial. The tube took a bit of time to warm up before it tried to show a newscast from a station in Poplar Bluff, but the greens were yellow and the blues were red and the volume was static. He cranked the 13-channel dial all the way around twice, hoping to find anything at all, yet no picture other than a snow blizzard appeared.

He shut off the tube and sat down on the couch and ran his fingers through his greasy scalp. He wondered how he might spend his second day in Doe Run, figuring it sure as hell couldn't be as discouraging as the first.

"Good for nothin' son of bitch," he cussed, remembering how his rotten daddy had not left even a pot for him to piss in.

As he lit his first Camel of the morning, his mind continued to ponder upon his dead daddy. He thought of how his shiftless father had once won a two hundred grand lawsuit from the local lead mine company by faking a spinal injury supposedly suffered on the job. He also remembered how his daddy had never forked over a dime of that lawsuit money to pay for a hospital bed for his dying wife, instead letting her shrivel into a black prune at home until she miserably died.

Yes sir, his rotten daddy was a no-good son of bitch, he concluded. A man who had never cared about any damn one or any damn thing except his own damn self. Now his only son would just have to find a fast job to gain enough cash to get the hell out of Doe Run again.

By the time he finished his cigarette and the ill thoughts of his rotten daddy had petered out from his memory, there was still no sign of Byron, so he headed back to the bathroom to clean up. It was bad enough he had to step into the scum-infested stall, but he also discovered the water heater was broken. He spent two godawful minutes scrubbing a bar of soap over his shivering body, all the while bawling cusses at the icy water trickling from the spout. He washed his greasy hair in the sink and followed up with a foamless shave that left red cuts on his face. Still, once he flung on a pair of clean jeans and clean wool sweater, he vainly surmised that the reflection in the mirror was much more handsome and presentable than his haggard appearance of yesterday.

With Byron still gone he got tired of waiting to eat, so he grudgingly took out the hunk of braunschweiger from the fridge. He sliced off a lump with a butcher knife and tossed it into a crusty skillet of hot grease on the stove, and after it had cooked, he wolfed it down with a pot of coffee he had brewed. Then with his belly satisfied and his spirits risen to the mood of content, he came to the decision that he was going to drive into town and see Tara Hawkins.

It was a little past noon by the time he made it to Doe Run and parked outside the Queenway Diner. He idled inside and found the place bustling with the lunchtime crowd and was told that Thursday is Tara's regular day off. Displeased by the news, he slumped down at a table and spent a few minutes browsing the menu. Then when the gullible wait-ress Stephanie asked for his order, he charmed her into tell-ing him Tara's address and left without ordering.

A drizzle of rain began to pepper the Firebird's wind-shield as he drove along Main Street. His eyes peeled at the passing cars, looking for a familiar face he might recall, and he found it a little eerie that the head of nearly every man driver was covered with a blaze orange hunting cap.

After crossing Grant Street then turning onto Fourth, he came to a small white building with a black cross and the words *Church of Christ* painted over its entryway. Next-door was a brown brick house with a screened-in front porch bellowing out into the yard. He pulled over to the curb and parked then got out of the car and hustled along through the light rain. As he bound up the porch steps, he felt his insides floating like a shy lad fixing to greet a pretty girl for a first date.

When he got to the door he paused to clear the butterflies with a raspy cough. Then he rapped a hard knock with his knuckles. Within a minute the door opened and out came a white-headed man beholding the affectionate beam of a soul saver.

Pen stood silent, perplexed by the old man's age.

"Yes?" said the kind preacher, charily studying him.

"Are you the preacher next door?"

"Yes I am."

Confusion rattled Pen's nerves.

"Is Tara stayin' here?"

"Yes. Yes, she is."

The preacher's response hung a tone of suspicion.

"Well, I'm an old friend of hers." Pen coyly looked behind himself, as if somebody was there coaching him. "She here now?"

"May I ask your name?"

"Pen Cullen."

"Oh." The preacher's wildly grown white eyebrows arched. "She's mentioned you, yes." He widened the door. "Come on in."

Pen had never stepped foot into a preacher's house before and he was surprised to find that it could have just as easily been the home of an appliance salesman. A comfy couch and two recliners and a color TV fitted the room, and nowhere to be seen was a painting of Lord Jesus or his corpse hanging on the cross. The only real sign of any religion at all was the thick Bible lying on an end table.

"Feels pretty cozy in here," Pen pointed out, nodding at the stove heater blowing air from the corner. The room must've been ninety degrees.

"My wife has poor blood circulation," the preacher explained. "She keeps us sweatin' like pigs in July."

"Your wife?"

"Yes."

Pen sensed a surge of relief stir through his guts. He suddenly felt foolish for believing that Tara had taken up with the old preacher man.

"Pen?"

The men turned their heads to behold Tara standing across the room. She was wet out of the shower, wearing a pink terry-cloth robe. Her stunned face was perfectly framed within the curling wet locks of chestnut hair cascading from the white towel twisted around her head.

"I stopped by the diner," Pen explained, as though it was a good enough answer for his surprise visit. His sight roamed down to her bare legs to her bare ankles to her bare feet and pink-tipped toes. "I thought maybe I'd see if you weren't as busy as you were yesterday."

"Jack?" called out a woman's voice from another room.

"Yes dear?" the preacher barked back.

"Where are those empty boxes we brought from the grocery store?"

"They're still in the car, unless you brung them in."

"Can you go out and get them?"

The preacher respectfully bowed his head. "Y'all have to excuse me. We're fixin' to take food to the elderly folks at the nursin' home." He patted Pen's shoulder. "Nice to meet you, son."

Pen's arm muscles constricted to the holy man's touch, but he remained cordial. "Good to meet you too, reverend."

"There's only one Reverend," the preacher corrected him, "and that's the Lord. Jack or Mr. Fox is fine."

After the preacher scuttled off to the kitchen, Pen and Tara remained eager and anxious, gawking at one another.

"Catch you at a bad time?"

"Not really." Her voice was shaky. She clasped at the collar of her robe. "Today's the day when we usually go share some company with folks that don't have long to live is all."

"What if I said that I didn't have long to live?" he remarked, jokingly. "Would you spare a little of yourself for me?"

"Maybe," she played along.

Goose bumps were shooting down her body, like they'd done when she was thirteen at the Junior High dance, and like they'd done when she was sixteen lying in the cramped seat of his '66 Chevy.

"I was thinkin' about goin' out to the house, see if there's anything worth gettin'," he said evenly, his voice turning low. "Wasn't sure I wanted to go there alone."

Tara recognized the hurt within his words. It was the same hurt of the motherless boy he used to be. She lowered her head and turned toward the kitchen, questioning if the preacher and his wife could hear them and were listening, then she looked back at Pen with sympathy in her eyes.

"Let me get dressed."

15

AS HE TURNED THE FIREBIRD onto Central Avenue, Pen snuck another glance at Tara's supple body and pretty face. Besides glossing her smile with red lipstick and powdering her cheeks and chin, she had plugged a couple of fake diamond studs into her lobes and hung a silver necklace with a crucifix around her neck. Her clothes were ass-tight faded denims on the bottom, a comfy red sweater with a navy-blue goose-down coat on the top, and on her little feet was a pair of chestnut Ropers.

Ever since they had pulled away from the preacher's house, both of them had been privately holding a bundle of varying emotions inside their chests. So far, he had only been able to brag about owning his dream car and had subtly mentioned that for the past couple of years he had been working construction jobs in Reno. All the while Tara had remained stiffly subdued and quiet in her seat with her nervous guts twisting and twisting.

"How's your sister?" he asked, flipping on the wipers to smooth out the rain dribbling across the windshield.

"Doin' fine," Tara anxiously replied. "She went off to college in Kansas City and ended up stayin' there. She married an eye doctor and they have little two girls."

"Two girls, uhh? That's hard to imagine."

"Yeah, she's changed quite a bit," Tara said with a slight smile. Then her graver thoughts spoke up. "Did you see Byron?"

Pen tossed her a side glance.

"Stayed with him last night."

"Is he okay?"

"Depends on what you mean by okay."

"Was he drinkin'?"

"We had a few beers. Didn't get to talk to him too much, I fell asleep pretty early."

"He shouldn't be drinkin' at all."

Pen detected spurn in her voice.

"So where else you been other than Reno?"

"Oh, lots of places."

"Like where?"

"Santa Fe. San Antonio. New Orleans. Miami. Other places that ain't much more than a spot on a map."

"Wow. That is a lot." Tara's nerves were easing, as she was sinking back to the young girl she once was. "Where'd you like it best?"

"Hadn't really ever considered any favorites. But every place grows on you a little, I guess."

"Come on. There's gotta be a favorite."

"Well, it sure as shit ain't Doe Run." He grinned.

She gave a little smirk back. He noticed it, and then his eyes again rolled over to see the red shine on her lips.

"So how'd you come to shacking up with the holy rollers?"

"There's not much to tell about it really." Tara had to work her nerves a moment before spilling it. "There were some ladies from the church who came to my door one day, and I told them my situation. Then a few days later, Mr. Fox came by and said I could come stay at his home till I was back on my feet."

"What situation was that?"

"Byron had stopped payin' on the house."

Again, he heard the spurn in her voice.

"It's hard to keep up a mortgage on waitress tips."

"Got to be pretty weird livin' with a preacher."

"They're just folks like anybody else."

"Except the no drinkin' and the no cussin' part?"

She smiled easily. "Except for those things, yeah."

"So you a true believer now?"

"I try to be."

"Well, I don't know too much about it, but if I happen to get to those pearly gates by accident, I have a whole list of gripes for the Big Man upstairs."

"It's more about forgiveness."

"Maybe that's the part I'm missin' then. All I know is that if all of us really are made in His image, then He must be a twisted bastard."

"That sounds like somethin' Byron would say," Tara replied, looking away to the rainy sights flashing by out the window.

Pen again detected the bitter sound in her voice, and he could only suspect the obvious.

"By ever. . . Get out of hand?"

Tara dropped her head and fell into a stunned awkwardness.

"There was just nothin' to hold us together after Jake was gone."

"That was your boy?"

"Jacob," she whispered and nodded.

"Must've been tough goin' through somethin' like that."

Tara could only purse her lips and look away as a response. Sensing her grief, Pen decided not to question her further about her busted marriage to Byron, or the dead child, or the other possible reasons behind the spurn in her voice. And so with no further subject to speak upon, they fell back into their separate silences as the steady rain peppered down on the windshield.

Byron had started sucking on the bottle of Ten High the second he had gotten back to his parked Ram on the log road in Osage Bend. It was now about one in the afternoon, and he was fairly drunk again.

Once he hit the streets of Doe Run, he steered directly to Virgil Stout's store on the corner of Ninth Street and Central Avenue, and he became disgruntled upon seeing too many damn trucks in the parking lot, driven by too many damn out-of-towners.

When he strolled inside the store, he glanced at Virgil Stout busy behind the counter. The tickled look on the old timer's bearded face told that he was thrilled by the booming business from the out-of-towners. Hunters from as far away as Iowa and Illinois were buying orange caps and orange vests and orange gloves and orange coats and orange coveralls. Some held hand warmers and insulated socks, and a couple of them were clashing plastic rattling antlers together. One was sniffing a bottle of fox urine.

Byron stepped in the nine-man deep line to the checkout counter, ignoring the chaotic conversations taking place around him. His attention stuck on the TV set near the store entrance. It was playing a video called *How To Land Big Bucks.* The color screen was showing two whitetail stags with their heads down and their shoulder muscles bulked, ready to smash skulls. He couldn't make out all the narrator's words, but the voice said something about how the dominant eight-point buck was defending its territory from a six-point rival. The narrator went on to explain that even though these clashes rarely ended in death, these battles of survival can cause serious injuries, such as a stab wound or a gouging of an eye, and although uncommon, cases have been found where the bucks' antlers had locked together and both animals had broken their necks by attempting to disentangle.

As the video played on and the line to the counter grew shorter, Byron managed to hold back from lashing out his annoyance toward the out-of-town hunters. It was hard. Since the death of his boy, he hated all people in general.

"You know the best way to get to Iron Springs?" he overheard a city hunter ask Virgil.

Virgil collected his thoughts for a moment and then gestured wide with his arms and hands to better explain the route. "Well first, you go out Highway W about twelve, thirteen miles, then you should see a sign that says Iron Springs. It's a left turn, best I remember."

"Is the hunting out there good as they say it is?"

"About as good as anywheres else, I reckon. Let's just pray this rain lets up or there ain't gonna be no good places to go."

Virgil rang up the cost of the city hunter's items and then noticed the bearded drunk standing next in line. "Well, I'll declare. Byron Tisdale? Is that you behind all that hair?"

Byron timidly nodded. "Yes sir."

"I was just talkin' about you yesterday." Virgil winked at the city hunter. "That there's the feller you wanna talk to. Shoot, he probably knows where the deer are hidin' better than anybody else in the whole county. Used to be game warden."

The city hunter turned and smiled courteously at the crystal-eyed hairy man. "You mind if I ask where you think the best place to hunt is?"

Byron shied away, disliking the sudden and unwanted attention forced upon him. But he managed to act civil and addressed the city hunter in a teasing manner. "Well, if I told you, word might spread around and I wouldn't get the one I got my eye on for myself."

Virgil and the city hunter shared a guffaw.

"But I seen pretty good bucks over there in Iron Springs, all right," Byron added, to cut the city hunter off from asking more questions.

"Thanks for the tip," replied the city hunter. He nodded friendly-like and collected his goods and went on his way.

Byron placed his driver's license on the counter. "I need a huntin' tag and a box of thirty-ought," he said hoarsely, already with a wad of cash out for a speedy buy.

"Okie-doke." Virgil bent down behind the counter where the ammo was stacked. "What grain you need?"

"Got one-thirty?"

"Sure do." Virgil came up with the right box in hand. "Got a big ole buck picked out, do you?"

"I's just funnin' the man."

Virgil began writing up the hunting permit and studied Byron's driver's license through his smeared bifocals.

"This here your correct address?"

"Most correct I got."

"I'll take your word for it," Virgil chuckled. "I ran into a feller named Cullen lookin' for you yesterday."

"He was askin' about me?" Byron snapped.

"I just happened to give him a lift into town when his car got stuck in the ditch. He's got hisself a sweet ride, one of 'em Firebirds I think he said it was."

Byron eased up. "Yeah, he found me,"

"Good, good. I bet it's got to be a little different for you this year, huh?"

"Whatta you mean?"

"Huntin' a buck yourself, instead of huntin' poachers."

"Ain't a whole lot of difference." Byron glanced at the TV set by the door. "Still gotta know where to find 'em."

Virgil smiled and finished writing up the permit and pointed the pen to a line on the paper.

"Just sign there and you're good to go."

Byron scrawled his name and paid the charges, raring to get the hell out of there.

"Well, good luck to you," Virgil offered.

Byron nodded, grabbed his purchases, and hurried for the door before anyone else tried to spark a neighborly conversation.

Once he was back outside, he hustled across the parking lot toward the Ram, and the second he plopped himself behind the driver's seat, he unscrewed the cap of the Ten High and chased off his heightened nerves. Then breathing hard, he cranked the engine up, tucking the bottle in his lap for emergency sips for the drive.

As he backed out of the filled lot, he nearly nudged into a couple of parked pick-ups. Then pulling the front end of the Ram around to face the street, he braked upon spotting the black Firebird cruise by in front of him. And sitting pretty in the passenger seat was his ex-wife.

16

THE CULLEN HOME WAS BUILT BACK IN '64 when the government began guaranteeing house loans to any penniless person who could scribble a signature on a deed. The godsend chance to own a new home had brought dozens of dirt-poor families from the backwoods and busted farmlands, and within two years' time the town of Doe Run had itself with a booming population of 2,183 souls.

Course not all the townfolks were pleased about the growth spurt. Most of the holier-than-thou families that had resided in town for the last half-century hated the idea of having backwoods beggars strolling the streets and ruining the school. But as with most hindrances of smalltown views, the Chamber of Commerce businessmen bitterly fought and won for the greedy prospect of increased revenues, so the backwoods beggars got to come and build their cheap home-steads in a new neighborhood, aptly deemed Newtown.

As Pen now steered the Firebird over the chug-holed streets of Newtown, he was dumbstruck by how the neigh-borhood had become such a rundown ghetto in less than thirty years. Course last spring's tornado greatly spurred it that way. Half the houses gave the impression that a dozer had crawled over them and whole trees lay uprooted and twisted in yards alongside scattered piles of ripped-apart sofas and mattresses and general trash.

"Damn," Pen exclaimed, staring at the destruction. "Looks like a train came off its tracks through here."

"It was really awful," Tara concurred. "It's a miracle only two was killed."

"Who was it?"

"Mark Tully and his wife Joy."

"The butcher at IGA?"

Tara nodded. "Yeah. It was a real shame cause they could've went to the armory for shelter. That's what a lot of folks who didn't have basements did when the sirens went off."

"I forget, which house they live in?"

"It was a couple blocks back that way," she answered, pointing eastward. "It's just rubble now though."

They drove on and arrived in front of the two-bedroom home where Pen had grown up, and upon first sight he wondered how his rotten daddy had suckered the bank into a second mortgage on the decrepit place. Half the roof shingles were shed and the dull gray vinyl siding was mottled with black mold and neon green moss.

He pulled the Firebird into the driveway and parked and shut off the motor. The rain was coming down in sheets and sounded like hail thumping the car.

"Looks like we're gonna get a little wet."

Tara curled a smile. "I won't melt."

They hopped out of the car and sprinted to the front door of the house. It was bolted shut with a padlock.

"Shit," he hissed. "Damn door's locked."

They both gauged the carport and its falling overhang, and after Pen nodded a mutual understanding to her, they hustled toward it to get out of the rain. Then standing there underneath it, she gazed at him for the next idea.

"Back door might be unlocked," he suggested. "Why don't you wait here while I go check."

"Okay."

He raised his leather jacket over his head and dashed around the side of the house.

When he made it to the backyard he sailed up to the backdoor and tugged on the handle. It too was bolted shut.

"Are you shittin' me?"

Vexed, he hopped over to a bedroom window and ripped down the rusted screen hanging loosely on its frame. He tried to lift the window open, but it wouldn't budge from its seal.

"Fuck!" he cussed, smacking the frame with his fist.

He staggered back a few steps, glaring at the window with bitter disgust. He then realized that he was standing on the reverse side of the glass he'd once stared out of as a dreaming boy. His mind's eye envisioned that same dreaming boy peering out and judging his older self, and the eerie vision spooked the hell out of him.

His eyes shifted away from the window and landed on a corroded and bent-up section of guttering that had fallen off from the roof's edge. He reached down and gripped it firmly in his hands. He stuck it straight out from his body, and like a cannon on wheels, he rushed toward the window and viciously rocketed it through. The glass exploded. And with it shattered the haunting remembrance of himself as a dreaming boy.

He shucked the guttering back to the muddy ground and

climbed upon the window frame to slip through. He was careful not to cut his hands on the broken shards, and after all of him fell inside, he found that the bedroom was bare. No bed. No pictures. Nothing but a grease-stained toolbox on the barewood floor and the stench of musty air.

He strolled out into the hallway and idled into the living room. He took a moment to take in the bareness of it all. Faded green wallpaper lost of its glue and whole sections slumped down to the floor. Crumples of plaster dropped from the water-stained ceiling. The same iron woodstove at the head of the room, with the same pair of horseshoes hanging upside-down on the wall above it. The same pea green couch he used to lay upon, its fabric split and its stuffing bellowed out. The same tan recliner in only slightly better condition. The worn caramel-colored carpet was splotched with black stains and bent soda cans and candy wrappers were littered in the corners. The only piece of furniture he hadn't seen before was the dusty TV stand absent of a TV.

He crossed to the front door and unlocked the handle, but the steel bolt was fixed firmly from the outside. He lifted his right foot and started punting, over and over, until the wood splintered apart, and after a few more solid stomps the door flew open.

He arched his head out from the doorway and waved for Tara to come in. She remained still for a moment, concerned by his violating the door, then she quick-stepped across the carport and bounced inside.

"Didn't nobody give you a key?" she asked, shaking the wetness off her goose-down coat and sock hat.

"I used what they gave me."

He flicked the light switch on the wall and glanced at

the lamp that stood leaning in the corner. The electricity was shot.

"Bank must've sent somebody to clean out anything of worth," he grumbled. "Used to do the same thing for them." His eyes read the room. "It's like I can still smell him in here."

"When's the last time you spoke to him?"

"Day I left."

Then as if he were in a necromancer's trance, he ambled out of the room and left her standing there alone.

He went down the hallway again, past his boyhood bedroom, and arrived at a door. He cracked it open with his fingers and peeped inside. He saw a king size mattress and box springs with no sheets or blankets. Though it was not the same bed his mom had breathed her last breath on, he could see her lying on it. He had never forgotten how she had looked during her last days. Shriveling like a discarded apple core. Her face shrinking into nothing more than wrinkled yellow skin. As a boy he could never bring himself to wander inside her room, and he still couldn't seem to brave enough courage now, and so he turned away from the door and went back down the hallway.

He came into the kitchen. His fingers ran across the dust that had settled on a scarred oak dining table. He stopped and studied the three matching chairs standing upright in the corner. The fourth was leaned against a wall, missing a leg.

He softly stepped across the sticky and torn linoleum, pausing to check inside the hickory cabinets. A couple of plastic ice cube trays stacked on the bottom shelf. A ball of string and a souvenir shot glass from Branson filled with tacks and screws.

He wandered to the fridge and opened it. More emptiness. Then his eyes came up to notice Tara step into the kitchen.

She stared at him with benevolent intent. Feeling sorry for his sorrow. The dull echo of the rain drumming on the rooftop making it all the more sorrowful.

"Why did you take off like you did?"

His eyes narrowed annoyance at her question.

"Do I really need to explain?"

"I was just wonderin' why you never came back."

"What the hell was there to come back to?"

Tara's eyes rolled downward.

He blew through his lips. Then he idled away from the fridge and walked on past her. Tara swallowed her nerves and followed behind him like a badgering shadow.

He stopped in the middle of the living room and looked down at the frayed carpet, trying to restrain the mad rush of bad memories hitting him. "I don't what I thought I would find here."

"Just because you left," her voice quavered. "Doesn't mean you didn't stay a part of here."

"I didn't want to be a part of here."

"Why?"

"Because the last time I stood right here, I thought I killed the son of a bitch!"

"I didn't mean to get you upset."

"Upset?" He turned around and snorted. "I'm just tellin' you why I left and never came back. That's what you asked, ain't it?"

She could sense his anger brewing.

"It doesn't matter."

"Sure it does."

She reached and touched his arm. But he couldn't let it go now that the black cat had been let loose from its bag.

"Came home from work from that sawmill job and he's here with one of those mouthy bitches he kept around, both of them drunk off their asses. Soon as I walked through the door, he went to yellin' at me. I didn't cut the goddamn grass or wash his car or who knows what the hell it was. I told him to leave me the fuck alone but hell if the fucker didn't go off and bust my head open with his goddamn ashtray."

He parted his hair with his fingers to show her.

"See the scar?"

Tara obliged him but was becoming more startled by his baneful words.

"Didn't have much of a choice after that, so I jumped on him and bashed his face with that fuckin' ashtray is what I did. Beat on him till he stopped movin'. Then that crazy bitch he was with started screamin' that she was gonna call the cops, so I ran out."

He looked at Tara and saw her wide-eyed and tense and hugging herself.

He swallowed, pushing down his ire.

"I figured the only thing to do was to leave town, but I had blood all over me, so I hurried over to that trailer Byron was livin' in to clean up first. Last thing I ever expected was seein' both of you wrapped up on the floor like you was."

"I'm sorry."

He saw the teardrops on her cheeks.

"We were barely more than kids," he huffed. "Besides, I didn't kill him."

She kept up the sobs. "It was all my fault."

Then she turned her face away so that he could no longer judge it.

Though he wasn't certain of the reason why, her theatrics were riling him. He stepped closer to her and grabbed her shoulders and spun her around to face him.

"Hey. What's wrong with you?"

Tara crumbled into his chest.

"Forgive me."

He could feel her flesh in a fiery fever and his arms yanked her away from his hammering heart. He recognized her soppy eyes begging for him to take her.

So his mouth sank into hers.

They fell back into a mislaid time of their shared past.

Their bodies clutching. Fumbling.

Then they found their way down onto the pea green couch.

His hands flew to the waistband of her denims. Her fingers reached inside his jeans and grabbed hold. He slanted over her. She guided him between her. His one hand clutching her chestnut hair, the other seizing her breast. She moaned. Her calves and ankles clamped around his waist. Her teeth bit his neck, stifling her screams. Time ceased as they jerked. Swayed. Grunting. Gasping. Traveling in suspension. Then their bones bowed and their strength squeezed in unison and they both cried out like two newborns stretching into the world for the first time.

They lay spent. Silent. Body to body. Catching breath. The rain pattering on the rooftop.

Finally, Pen stood from the couch and lifted his pants up from his boots.

Tara watched him, saying nothing.

She reached for her denims and panties lying on the floor, and like a gentleman he picked them up and handed them to her.

"Thanks," she whispered.

She began slipping back into her jeans, not looking at him. Taken by hollow shame.

"I need to go to the bathroom."

"Probably don't flush," was his reply.

She trotted out of the living room.

He patted his jacket for a Camel and sat back down on the couch. He lit up and deeply inhaled, hoping the fumes would flatten the lumps mounting inside his stomach.

The rain from outside drummed louder. Yet he could still make out the faint sobs of her crying coming from down the hallway, behind the bathroom door.

17

THE HEAVY DOWNPOUR HAD RETREATED to a dying drizzle by the time they got back into the Firebird and drove away from Pen's childhood home. As they rode through the Newtown streets, neither one knew how to speak about what had happened. He wanted to make a light-hearted comment. Like maybe they could just chalk it up to Mother Nature, no different than beasts in the fields, birds in the wind, or fish in the seas. But his wiser sense knew better than to speak flippantly about it. So instead, "Glad to see this rain let up," mumbled out of him.

"I've got sort of used to it comin' and goin'," she replied, her voice disconnected from the impure thoughts running wild inside her head.

"Anywhere you wanna go?"

"I should probably get back home." She tried to smile away her lust and shame. "Tonight's my night to fix supper."

Pen took her response as her way of saying that she desired to be alone, yet he also wondered how he would answer if she asked him to eat with her and the holy rollers. He wasn't capable of handling that kind of scene right now. Right now, he needed a scene with several strong drinks in it.

The rest of the ride to the preacher's house was a silent one, and when he braked the Firebird in the driveway neither one of them were certain how to entertain an apt goodbye. He waited for her to say something pure and kind. Something like it was nice to see you again, or don't be a stranger, or something to that effect. One of those suitable so longs a Christian woman would say.

"So you gonna stay with Byron again?" she asked, which was not at all a question he was expecting.

He shrugged. "Maybe."

Her chin bowed down to her neck as if she had a deep personal thought, and then she jerked the door latch and pressed the car door open with her forearm. Once her right foot arched and hit the pavement, she twisted back around and stared intensely into his face like she was getting ready to set a buried secret free.

But she didn't know how to say it.

Instead, she leaned over the console and gently kissed his lips. She then turned and hurried out of the car, darting across the yard and up the porch stairs.

Pen watched her bound up the steps and escape behind the front door until she was completely gone from sight. He exhaled and wiped his nose with his sleeve. His eyes popped to the rearview. He tugged the collar of his sweater back from his throat and saw the purple bite marks she'd left near his neckline.

For the next hour, he wheeled the Firebird from one end of town to the other, inhaling Tara's scent to not lose the fresh memory of holding her in his arms again. It had come so unexpected, yet expected. So unreal, yet more than real. And as he was remembering her naked and pure on that pea green couch, he had to force himself to leave the streets before he rushed to the preacher's house again and bade her for more.

It was close to four o'clock by the time he was easing the Firebird down the high hill slope overlooking Joe's farm. The dying sun was hidden behind low and heavy clouds, but there was still enough daylight to make out the shape of the rusted Ram and the whiff of smoke puffing out from the stone chimney of the cabin.

He drove up and parked and shut the engine off but remained in the driver seat to finish his cigarette. A strange feeling was thrumming through him. A kind of pride. Like he'd won a prize. Then after killing the Camel butt, he hopped out of the car, and bursting with bold brashness stepped inside the cabin.

He smartly called out loud and clear, "Hey By? It's me," not yearning to be met with a fire poker up the side of his skull. No answer came back. But he could smell the faint reek of skunk. He treaded softly into the kitchen, noticing store-bought food on the counter. Six cans of pork and beans and six cans of stew. A couple tins of tuna and a box of saltine crackers.

"By? You around?" he called out again.

"In here," came a gruff response from the living room.

Pen again felt the strange surge of pride rising in his chest when he heard the bark of Byron's voice. He had an itch to waltz in there and brag how he'd spent the afternoon fucking Tara. But the notion died when he ambled into the living room to see Byron working the Redfield scope onto a thirty-ought-six Winchester.

"Well damn, look at you, killer." Pen's eyebrows lifted crookedly. "Got somethin' goin' on I should know about?"

"Just gettin' ready to hunt."

"Good God. Is every sum bitch who can shoot a gun sideways aimin' to kill Bambi this weekend?"

"Folks just like to kill shit when the chance comes."

Pen noticed the remains of the joint he had left in the ashtray last night. It was now burned down to a paltry roach.

"Smoke a little green bud while I was gone, did you?"

Byron peeked up, his crystal gray irises spinning in pink balls. "Didn't figure you'd mind."

"I must've passed out on you last night." Pen pinched the roach into his fingers and took the Zippo from his pocket. "You have yourself an eventful day?"

"No different than most." Byron picked up his half-gone bottle of Ten High and obliged himself to a swallow.

"Be careful," Pen warned, "that shit will put you six foot low."

He lit the roach and let the smoke rush inside him.

Byron ignored the friendly advice and took another swallow then put the bottle down. Then he leaned for a big cardboard box on the floor and grabbed a ripped-up rag from it. As Pen watched him, his mind suddenly recalled how his plan of picking up his family inheritance had gone bust. He took another hit to squash the upsetting thought.

"What'cha got in there?"

"Just some huntin' stuff."

Pen stepped over and stooped down to rummage through the box. On top lay a can of gun cleaning spray, along with a cleaning rod and strips of soiled rags. He dug around and found spare bullets of various calibers and a couple of broken rifle scopes, and at the bottom of the box was a pair of yellow-tinted shooting glasses.

"All this shit yours?"

"Belonged to some city assholes that Joe let come out here and hunt. One of the stupid fuckers shot his dog."

"On purpose?"

"Just dumbass ignorance."

"What kind of dog?"

"Black Lab."

"Zorro?"

"Same one."

"Damn, that dog lived a long time."

"Joe was about ready to slit the throat of the fucker who shot it, but the guy offered this thirty-ought as forgiveness." Byron nudged his chin toward a heavy muslin grain sack sitting in the corner. "The others he's with was so damn scared, they left all this shit and took off."

Pen went over and lifted the sack. "Jesus." It landed back onto the floor with a thud. "What all the hell's in here?"

"I ain't never looked through it all."

Pen knelt closer to pilfer inside. He pulled out a couple of blaze orange vests and a pair of orange cotton gloves spotted with dried blood. Next came out a blaze orange ski mask and he stuck his fingers through its eye holes and mouth.

"Did I tell you I ran into a doe yesterday? Comin' into town?"

"Naw, I don't think so."

"Fuckers are a nuisance."

Pen peeped up to see Byron obsessively working the scope on the gun. He dared himself to say something about Tara. But his sentimental side warned him not to spoil his somewhat repaired camaraderie with his old buddy, especially since he was dead broke with nowhere else to go.

"There any drinkin' establishments left in town?

"Only place is The Hoghead.

"Hoghead?"

"Used to be Tin Horn Saloon."

"That pisshole on Broadway?"

"Same one."

"That's the only place?"

"Since Webster's Bar closed."

Pen shook his head over the severe lack of possibilities to have a good time and forget his troubles. He wandered over to the window and pulled back the curtains to peer out into the dreary sky. The horses and the jack were standing like marble statues out in the field.

"How long's Joe had them skinny ass horses?"

"Four, five years."

"Anybody ever ride them?"

"Not that I know of."

"Thought maybe he's tryin' to become a *vaquero*."

"He just bought 'em to have somethin' to do."

"Must suck havin' fences around you like that. I'd rather somebody put me out of damn misery."

Pen turned from the window and studied his old friend. He recognized the fat kid called Spook in him and he felt halfway sorry for the sorry bastard.

Byron peeped up from his work on the rifle, his doped-up orbs the color of raw steak. "What'd you say?"

Pen smiled and shook his head. "Nothin', man." He moved away from the window and flicked the roach into the fireplace. "Why don't we get out of these woods? Take a ride in my 'Bird. Maybe hit this tavern or some shit."

"Don't need to go to town for a drink."

"Well what else are we gonna do? Play cards?"

Byron rubbed his squinty eyes. His paranoid self told him that it might make sense to show his face in town so folks wouldn't suspect how crazy he'd become. Folks were probably already whispering about his oddball behavior, just like they had done with his insane mother.

"You got any more of that weed?"

"I got a little." Pen winked and grinned.

18.

PLOP.

Plop.

Plop.

Tara had been stretched in the tub for over two hours. The snowy bubbles had long been popped by the drips falling from the faucet, and her smooth skin had shriveled up like a wet prune. Still, she didn't believe the baptism had washed away her lustful sins. Her body could feel him on her. Feel him inside of her.

Plop.

Plop.

Plop.

A cold shiver shot through her nakedness and broke her meditation. She propped herself up and pulled the drain plug and twisted on the hot valve. She lay back down again to accept the warm stream onto her ankles and feet. She hugged herself with her goosebump arms. Her eyes closed. She listened to the cascading water. Then her mind fell back to thinking about the hows and whys she had become such a deceitful woman to the two men who had loved her.

It was the summer she turned eighteen. Her monthly blood flow had gone four weeks late. She dared not tell anyone of her predicament, especially her folks, knowing they would punish themselves for raising an impure daughter. Neither would she take a rabbit test to find out if the stork was coming because she didn't want to face the hard truth herself. Bearing a child would mean grown-up responsibility, and grown-up responsibility would mean that she couldn't elope with Pen, and if she couldn't run away with him, then she'd rather die.

So while the summer days passed with the child growing inside her womb, she began to lose hold of her sensible mind. First, she convinced herself that Pen's impulsion to get away from his cruel father ran much deeper than his many promises to her, and she feared that he would escape like a thief in the night, with or without her, child or not, if he ever suspected there was a trap set to ensnare him in Doe Run.

She began to vomit in the mornings. At other times she flew into the unpredictable moods any unwed gal with female troubles might entail. Then after a couple more weeks passed and still no female blood had flowed, she turned dire enough to see what the rabbit would say. The bunny said yes, so she asked two more, and when those bunnies agreed, she fell further into maddening bursts of despair.

That same long and hot summer, Byron had moved into a double-wide trailer to gain a nominal sense of independence from his insane mother and absent father. On the night Tara came to visit him, he was in a great deal of pain and fairly zonked on Vicodin, as earlier in the day at the sawmill he had dropped a log on his foot and broken a toe. Usually, he didn't appreciate visitors, but his attitude abruptly changed once he hobbled to the knock at his door and saw that it was Tara. Her eyes were welled-up and red as ripe tomatoes, and her voice cracked that she needed to talk to him. So he let her in and led her to the creaky rocking chair that his crazy mother had given him for his move out of the nest.

Dramatic tears bucketed down her puffy cheeks when she began to blubber how she'd gotten cold feet on her and Pen's planned elopement to Memphis. Between her sobs she said that she couldn't bring herself to secretly run away from her family--which wasn't a complete black lie since she had all but fooled herself into believing that was the real reason she couldn't leave. She told Byron how terrified she was of losing Pen forever. How she wouldn't be able to breathe without Pen in her life. How nothing in this whole wide world was more important to her than being with Pen Cullen for all her tomorrows and tomorrows. She couldn't make a choice between a stable life with her family here in Doe Run or an uncertain future with Pen away from her home, it wasn't fair for anyone to be asked to choose such a thing. She asked Byron if he might help her convince Pen into not leaving at all, talk some sense into him, talk him into staying so they could all be together like it had always been.

Byron played his sympathy well. He nodded his under-standing and mumbled *uh-huh* at the right intervals of her staggered speech. He then suggested she calm her nerves with some sips of a strawberry wine cooler, though he didn't admit that he only kept the sugary booze in the fridge for the off chance of bringing a loose gal over to screw.

She was so far gone in her brokenhearted delusions that she obliged his offer, with no concern to her pregnant condition. And after she drank four fast bottles, she was drunker than she'd ever been.

It was then that Byron became comfortable enough to speak a few humble words of his own. He claimed that he'd already tried to discourage Pen from splitting town, as he too would miss his only friend, but he had learned long ago that once Pen's mind was made up about something, not even a whole sky of wishing stars could bend his stubborn ways.

The dour outlook was not the encouragement Tara had come there to find. The two of them sat for a short while in wordless dejection. Then without any further prompting he swallowed the dry spit stuck in his throat and gathered the nerve to come out with what he'd always been too chicken-shit to say.

He admitted how he had been forced to grow up as a protector for his batshit crazy mother, rather than being raised as a normal son. He detailed how his hardened father had tried to instill within him a stern attitude against women, mainly that they were impulsive bitches capable of destroying any man. On and on he went with his pitiful confessions, prattling his remorse like a captured bandit headed for the hanging tree. His cheerless upbringing. His isolation. His nervousness around crowds. Then with a more soothing timber in his voice he confessed to not ever longing for any particular girl before. He'd kissed a few here and there, hideous gals with no better options, and he could only make-believe what it might be like to stick it out with a special girl for a lengthy stretch.

The tranquility of his melodious words mixed with the rush of the bubbly booze and sent her to an even more bewildered state. And it was then that he kneeled to her lap and gazed up at her face like a dutiful pet. His crystal gray eyes sparkled like crushed diamonds as he told her how much he appreciated her for treating him with kindness, and he swore that he'd not let her go feeling lonesome, if she ever did find herself alone. He promised to take care of her, like he'd cared for his momma, and in time, in time, if she might consider, if she might possibly like him as more than just a friend, well then, he'd be all right with that too.

When his calloused hand reached and cupped her wet cheek, she couldn't stop herself from rushing and sobbing her sadness into his arms. He petted her soft brown hair and let her cry. Then after a few moments of their touching embrace, he gently lifted her off the rocking chair and nudged her teary face back with his stubbly chin. They stared into one another, adrift in a churning world of loneliness and puzzlement. She was weak and drunk and incapable of thwarting the fingers of fate clutching at her better judgment, and so she didn't voice no or turn away when his mouth came to meet hers. Nor did her limp arms or her limp legs reject his intention when he took her to the floor.

His movements were jumpy and ungraceful, not at all gratifying to her. More like a jerky Ferris wheel ride that roils stomachs at the fair. Still, his lust was enough to liberate her caged torment, the worries over birthing Pen's child floated away from her mind like drifting dust, and the heaving and buckling upon her body shook her senseless until Byron's seed spilled inside of her.

Once it was done, they remained arrested in an awry shape of bonded flesh on the floor. Then a jiggling came from the door. Their heads arched up from their necks and they both glimpsed a familiar face stretch inside the open doorway. It was bruised and splattered with blood, and it morphed into an even more monstrous mug when it saw them together.

No words passed. Only stares of shame and regret. Then the blood-soaked visitor placed his borrowed key on a table beside the entrance and eased back from the open door and stepped out of their lives.

19

BLACK IN BLACK WAS SCREAMING from the back speakers as Pen steadied the Firebird along a half-mile straight stretch of Highway 21. He glanced over at his wasted passenger who was sucking from a bottle of Ten High and watching the darkness blur by outside the window.

"Hold on to your ass, mother fucker."

Then he gunned the gas.

The next bend of the road came up fast. Pen again peeped over to Byron and winked mischievously, as though he was daring to fly off the highway, and then right as they hit the bend he let off pedal and gripped the wheel and guided the Firebird tightly around the wide curve with the keen precision of a hawk diving down to earth to scoop up its scampering prey.

"Like a goddamn rocket, ain't she?"

Byron clumsily pulled the seat belt over his gut and clicked it. Pen cackled and howled, and on they rode.

By the time they hit town and were cruising down deserted Lincoln Boulevard they'd already burnt three joints down to roaches. Pen dropped the speed to dodge any town cop's attention and pulled up and parked in front of an old brick building on Broadway. A corroded neon sign above its door blinked *The Hoghead Tavern.*

As quick as the engine cut, Byron crawled out of the car, swallowing the backwash remains of his Ten High, then he chucked the bottle across the street.

Pen huffed with amusement. "Ready to go get drunk?"

Byron nodded with a guttural burp. Then the two old buddies swayed toward the tavern door and went inside.

The decoration was standard redneck fare. On the wall hung three buck heads, six largemouth bass, a stuffed wild boar, and a diversity of beer posters with bikini-clad women. The absence of clear light and the stench of booze, smoke, and piss added to the dreary atmosphere.

"What a shithole," Pen mumbled, questioning if coming here to enliven the night was the right play. He peeped at Byron who was wearing the droll face of a worried kid who'd just stepped into a funhouse of scary clowns.

Besides the rank decor, tonight wasn't looking like a hopping night, though the eight patrons scattered around the room might be considered a good haul for a Thursday. A trio of them were out-of-town hunters who'd stopped by to wet their whistles before hitting a lonely campfire. A couple of others were local boys off work from a chicken farm who'd come for a liquor buzz before heading home to their own hen houses. The remaining three were daily regulars, hunched over like a crew of buzzards on stools at the bar. One had milky eyes. A second could've been either man or woman, it was hard to discern in the darkly lit room. The third had a missing ear that looked like it'd been gnawed off by a Rottweiler.

"Come on in, boys," yelled the bartender named Sally, her voice clanging like a banjo. "Git ye selves a seat."

Pen and Byron heeded her call and strolled over and bellied up to the bar next to the drunk with the milky eyes.

"What can I get ye?" Sally posed, wiping the scarred bar counter with a stained towel.

"Two shots of Beam and two Buds," Pen ordered.

"Sure thang darlin'," she replied, grinning a row of buck teeth with one incisor missing. Under the flickering lights, they saw that she was a hideous three-hundred-pound creature with a pasty-white face cratered like the moon and an uneven mop of greasy black hair plastered on her colossal dome. Her massive girth was stuffed inside pink sweatpants and a black Harley Davidson shirt. Pen figured her to be some human byproduct born by a depraved burst of backwoods family lust.

"Is 'at you Byron Tisdale?" she rang out.

"Hidy," he grumbled, shyly bowing his hairy face.

"Well hell's bells, I ain't seen hide nor hair 'a ye in a coon's age. How ye keepin' ye self?"

"Gettin' along alright."

"Good to hear, good to hear."

That was the extent of their exchange. Byron was now even more hesitant to speak than usual since acute paranoia from the weed had hit his liquored brain.

Sally popped the caps on a couple of cold brews. Her pudgy fingers then groped two shot glasses and placed them onto the bar. "Y'all need mugs?"

"Bottle's good," Pen answered, catching sight of the one-eared drunk to his left. As she poured Jim Beam into the shot glasses, he took a sip from his beer. "You run us a tab?"

"Sure thang." She pointed to her fat head. "Hold it right here upstairs."

"Well add ten bucks worth of quarters for the jukebox. This place could use a little livin' up." He picked up one of the filled shot glasses and passed it to Byron.

"Cheers."

They chinked and chugged.

As Pen washed down the bite of Beam with a swallow of beer, he glanced at the three hunters conversing at a corner table. He speculated how he might shark them into a few games of friendly pool to spring for his drinking tab. Somebody was going to have to pay, and he knew it wasn't going to be him. He wiped sweat beads off his bottle with his thumb and looked back at Byron.

"You ever had a microbrew?"

"A what?"

"A microbrew. It's a kind of homemade beer."

"Can't say."

"Out in California and other places they got these fancy bars called microbreweries. It's pretty high-dollar beer and makes you sick as a pukin' dog if you have too many. Every time I find myself in one, I end up arguin' with the bartender that they ain't gonna ever make nothin' better than this homebrew right here." He held up his Budweiser bottle and pointed his finger to each letter of the famous name on the label--

"Because

yoU

Deserve

What

Every

Individual

<u>S</u>omeday
<u>E</u>ventually
<u>R</u>eceives."
He grinned wide and took a taste from his bottle.

Byron studied the label on his own bottle. "Sounds like a death sentence." Then tilted it to his lips.

Sally had been observing the grammar lesson and was gaping at Pen like he'd just enlightened her on the meaning of her own ignorant existence.

"How'd ye figure 'at out like 'at?"

"Fella named Bud told me," Pen answered her, straight-lipped. "He was wiser than most."

"Sheeit," she blushed. "Ye's a funny rascal ain't ye? Would ye write 'at down for me?"

"Well, I'm not so sure I'm willin' to give my secrets away for free."

Sally's face fell like a little girl who dropped her ice cream cone in the dirt. "Ye won't? Why not?"

"Hell, I'm just pullin' your leg."

"Really?" She beamed with her snaggletooth smile.

"Really."

"Let me get'cha a pen and paper."

As she wobbled to the cash register, Pen leaned toward Byron and whispered, "Reckon she can even read?"

"It's a damn wonder she can talk half right," the one-ear drunk muttered to them. "She's a licker, too."

"A what?" Pen asked back, hearing the man.

"A licker. Licks pussy."

"Likes the ladies, does she?"

"She's got to get it someplace." He thumbed his milky-eyed friend. "Even this blind dog here won't stick his dick in that tub of lard." He then busted out laughing.

Pen ignored the drunk lunatic as Sally returned and placed the pen and paper in front of him.

"Didja figure 'at out by ye self?"

"I done said, a wise fella named Bud told me."

"Now you stop ye foolin' me, I ain't as dumb as I look."

"Tell you what," Pen said while scrawling down the words for her. "I'll let you tell anyone you want that you came up with it yourself if you give me two more shots of Beam and a couple of those Swisher Sweet cigars up there on your shelf. On the house."

"Shoot. . . You sure are a rascal. Where'd ye find this 'un, Byron?"

"I don't claim him."

"Okay ye funny rascal," she agreed. "But don't ye go hollerin' to no one after ye drank it."

It was then two local gals pedaled through the door. One was brown-haired and wearing a fake cheetah coat. The other was a chunky dyed-blonde who had seen her better days. Both were dolled-up in ass-tight jeans and their faces were thickly caked in makeup and shiny lip gloss.

As they swayed across the room, they batted easy glances to the male prospects until their sights settled on the good-looking stranger sitting next to Byron Tisdale. They then made a big ordeal of it when they took off their coats and arched their backs and slid their rounded rumps into the chairs at a table.

"We'll take two Buds, Sally," the brown-headed one yelled out, her eyes staying on the devilish-handsome stranger.

"Be right with ye," Sally roared back, laying two Swisher Sweet cigars on the bar and dispensing another round of Beam.

"Thank you." Pen slid the paper that he'd written on

toward her. "I won't kid you no more. Truth is, the fella who told me was the king of beers."

"Oh! You get outta here," Sally snickered, turning away from him to get the two ladies their drinks.

"You know them?" Pen asked, nudging Byron in the arm.

"Who?"

"Peaches and cream who just walked in."

"Val Stockton and Trish Barnes."

"The cheerleaders?"

"Same ones."

Pen glanced over his shoulder at the two gals and saw that they were peeking back at him.

"Didn't you try to fuck one of 'em?"

"No."

"Which cheerleader was it then?"

"You're thinkin' of the flag girl in the marchin' band."

"That's right. What was her name?"

"Debbie Hood."

"Debbie Hood."

Pen chuckled. Then the funniness turned bitter when he considered that Tara had allowed herself to put out for the crazy bastard.

Byron chugged down his beer. "Gotta take a leak," he mumbled. Then he leaned from the bar and wandered off to the restroom.

Pen tipped his bottle to his lips as he kept wondering how long he could keep up his good graces toward his old friend. He again peeped at the two cheerleaders. They were chattering to themselves and the brown-headed one was pointing at him with her fake fingernails.

He gazed up at the stuffed boar on the wall. Then the

images of holding Tara on that pea green couch today began flashing in his mind.

20

THE JUKEBOX TUNES AND THE ROUNDS had kept coming. The hunters and the chicken ranchers had left, but the three barflies were still hanging on for last call. And the two buddies had somehow found themselves sitting at the table with the two cheerleaders.

The two chatty women had been providing the conversation, droning on and on about their shitty lives. How they'd moved to other no-name towns, how they were both stuck back in Doe Run after divorcing their worthless ex-husbands, and how they'd left their little ones with the grandfolks tonight so they might find a good time with the eightball of crank they'd scored today.

Pen had given them little notice and few words. His only aim was to have them pay for the booze bill. He had mostly stayed slumped in his chair, brooding over his grim existence, and was now trying to listen to Marty Robbins croon about a wicked Mexican woman at a El Paso cantina. Byron was in no better shape. He was sitting like a dead stump, hallucinating on the bubbles inside his beer bottle, and obsessing over the sack of shit who had scattered corn at his hunting spot.

"Sing it, Pen" cackled Trish, the brown-headed one.

"Yeah, get up and give us a show," Val chimed in.

He realized that he was slurring the verses of the song. He threw an evil eye at them, annoyed that they had interrupted his memory of Joe Silva introducing him to the whole chamber of Marty Robbins gunfighter ballads.

"Gotta pay me first."

He grabbed his half-smoked cigar from the table and flamed it while Trish leaned closer to him and stroked his inner leg with her fake nails.

"Got another one of those?"

He acted like she wasn't there and blew a smoke ring across the table. "Nope. By does. There in his pocket."

Val put her arm around Byron's neck. "Can I have it?" she chirped, pulling the cigar from his shirt pocket.

Byron squinted at her. Unsure of what she wanted or what she was doing or who she was.

Val took the Swisher Sweet and stuck it into her mouth. Pen was glad to see there was something to shut it the hell up.

"Can you light me?"

He leaned and reached his Zippo toward her face.

"Puff on it."

"Oh, she knows how to puff," Trish added.

"Only because you showed me how," Val cracked back, sucking on one end of the cigar to ignite the cherry on the other.

"You two sure are a couple of Chatty Cathies." Pen shut the flame from the lighter. "You've talked more to us the past five minutes than you did all four years of high school."

"We did too!" Trish disagreed.

"Bullshit. You were too busy shakin' your asses for the basketball team."

"Just because we didn't hang out with you don't mean we never talked to you," Val argued.

"And I remember you havin' Tara Hawkins around your neck all the time," Trish added with her lips curled up. "Maybe I didn't want to impose."

"Trish!" Val exclaimed. "Don't be so fuckin' crude!" Her eyes bulged and rolled toward Byron.

"That's his wife," she whispered.

"Oh." Trish giggled. She brought her hand out from under the table to cover her dirty mouth. "Sorry. I forgot."

Pen glared at her clown makeup face. He wanted to squeeze and crush it like an egg.

"Let's get outta here," Byron spoke up.

"Why?" Val asked. "You tired of us?"

"You're not wantin' to go cruisin' for teenage teases like every other good for nothin' in this town are you?" Trish spouted, her hand moving to Pen's leg and gripping him not to go.

Pen bore his eyes at Byron. Having these crank bitches talk about what he used to have with Tara was pushing him further into saying something that needed to be said.

"I'm not so sure a young gal can handle what Byron's got stored in his barn."

"What's that?" Val snickered. "A fireman's hose?"

"Let's get out of here," Byron slurred. His head was weaving out of rhythm with his dancing eyeballs.

"No, stay. Let's have another round," Trish begged.

"Hey Sally, bring us another round," Val yelled out.

"Sure thang," the ugly bartender called from the bar, her sight not leaving the TV.

Pen kept his drunken stare on Byron. That strange pride rising in his guts couldn't be held down any longer. "I ain't so sure no one knows this but me, but Byron used to have a little problem with his manhood. He couldn't get it up high enough to reach the sink you might say."

"He ain't the only one," Val cackled.

"Cheers to that," Trish agreed, raising her empty beer.

Pen blew smoke across the table.

"He's good now though, ain't you, By?"

Byron lofted his head from side to side, trying to figure out where he was.

"A few years back, I was livin' down in Texas workin' on an oil rig and heard this guy talkin' about some special techniques they have in Mexico to cure physical ailments that ain't allowed here in the states. Voodoo sort of shit. So knowin' about By's situation, I called him up, thinkin' he might be able to solve his little problem, and sure enough, he came on down to Texas to see me and we headed straight for the border to see that doctor."

"What'd you do, fill him up with Spanish Fly?" Val laughed.

"No, this was somethin' a little more complex." Pen lifted his beer bottle and drank the remains and put it back down. "Now this may sound a little weird, but what this Mexican doc did was, he sewed a baby elephant trunk on By's little dick. Like a sleeve."

"You are so full of shit," Trish giggled hard.

Byron reached for his shot of Beam and found it empty, oblivious to Pen raking him across the coals.

"He was sore for a week or so, but after he got his stitches out, we got him set up with this hooker from Houston to try it out. He didn't tell her about his surgery, but he paid her enough, so she'd be game for whatever. And to make her feel more comfortable before tellin' her about this operation on him, he took her to this real nice restaurant, like it was a real date or somethin'. One of those fancy joints where a steak will set you back a day's pay."

"Hold on," Trish interrupted him. She turned toward the bar. "You gettin' that round, Sally?"

"Hold your horses," Sally barked back. "It's comin'."

"Sorry. Go ahead."

Pen dumped ash from his cigar into the ashtray, his eyes mean on Byron. "Well, everything was goin' along just fine at the restaurant, this hooker was likin' By's company and all, laughin' at his jokes, and he's gettin' pretty excited in his pants, if you know what I mean. Well then all of sudden, as they were sittin' there talkin', this goddamn baby elephant trunk reaches up onto the table and grabs a breadstick, then boom!!"

Pen slapped his hand on the table.

Trish and Val jumped.

"It disappeared."

The women giggled.

"Course, Byron knew what it was, but he couldn't control that baby elephant trunk no more than he could control his little dick, and he got so goddamn embarrassed, all he could do was sit there and bow his head and cough, act like nothin' happened. But this hooker, shit, she freaked the plum out, and yelled 'What the fuck was that?!' Well about that time, this baby elephant trunk crawled right smack dab on the table again, grabbed another breadstick, then boom!" Pen's hand hit the table again. "It was gone."

The girls giggled more. Pen watched Byron grope an empty beer bottle and start sucking on it like a hungry baby.

Sally stepped up with four Budweisers clutched in her beefy claws and set the bottles down on the table.

"Here's ye beers, I'll be right back with ye shots."

"Thank you, Sally," Trish told her.

Back over at the bar, the one-eared drunk had stopped muttering to himself to better hear Pen's tall tale. His tongue rolled over his dry lips when he noticed the cold beers the foursome just received.

"Well By couldn't just ignore what this baby elephant trunk was doin', so he told the hooker all about the problems he'd been havin' with his little dick and all, and how he'd had this special operation. It was tough for him. Hell, look at him. Does By look like the kind of man who'd be comfortable with talkin' about that sort of thing to a woman?"

"Not really," Val chuckled.

"Well, thankfully this hooker was true professional, she even felt a little sorry for him, and she was sort of intrigued by the thought of a baby elephant trunk. I mean it might be a baby's, but it was still plenty damn big. So instead of gettin' freaked out like most women would've done, she leans in close and whispers to him, 'Well that must've been awful painful for you, but it does sound pretty exciting.' Then Byron says back to her, 'Well it ain't half as painful or nearly as excitin' as it's gonna be when I get up out of this goddamn chair and walk across this restaurant with these fuckin' breadsticks stuck up my ass.'"

The cheerleaders' laughter barreled across the tavern as Pen stretched his drunken smile, and they all got so carried away with laughing that none of them had noticed the one-eared drunk had shuffled up to their table and had snaked a beer, or that Byron had jumped out of his coma to slap the bottle out of the thief's mouth, and by the time the glass shattered on the floor, and Pen and the gals had finally caught to what was going on, Byron's hands were clenched around One-ear's neck and he was viciously hammering his head onto the table.

Bam. Bam. Bam.

Pen leaped straight up out of his seat while the cheerleaders screamed and scattered like quail.

Bam. Bam. Bam.

One-ear's face was morphing into a purple gourd.

Bam. Bam. Bam.

"Byron!" Pen bawled out. "Fuck man, let him go!"

But Byron's mind was gone somewhere in the peaks and valleys of dope and booze.

Bam. Bam. Bam.

With no other alternatives to stop the violence, Pen stepped in and took hold of Byron's big fist and tried to pull it off from squeezing whatever shitty life was left in the one-eared bastard.

"Byron! Enough goddamnit! Byron!"

Then here came ugly Sally into the fracas with a Louisville Slugger raised over her shoulder. "Turn him loose before I bash ye head in!"

Pen sprang backwards, not wanting to be thumped by Sally's swing, and when he stood back, he saw the same murderous gleam in Byron's eyes that was there when the fourth-grade version of him had nearly beaten Kenny Pruitt to death on the playground.

"I said turn him loose!" Sally warned again.

Fearing Byron's brains were fixing to be splattered by the bat, Pen lowered his shoulder and charged.

The collision was solid. Byron staggered back and his deathly grip loosened from One-ear's throat.

"Fuck you!" Byron roared.

Then he spewed vomit to the floor.

"Good God!" Sally bawled.

Byron made for another beer bottle and broke off its body with a slam on the table edge. He held out the shared glass in his hand like a Bowie knife, his crystal eyes blinking at the fat haint he could see clutching a bat.

"Get away from me!!"

Val screamed louder. Trish cowered behind a chair. The drunk who might've been a woman made a dash for the door, and the one with the milky eyes gaped open-mouthed from his stool.

Pen spat a gob of blood from his cut mouth and glared at his drunk friend.

"Put that damn bottle down!"

Byron's knees were buckling like a punch-drunk boxer on the ropes. "I'll kill you!" he crossly replied, coughing up hot bile stuck in his throat. "I'll kill you!"

Sally raised the bat higher over her shoulder, ready to swing a grand slam across Byron's brow.

"Put down the bottle, Byron!" Pen warned again.

No one moved. No one breathed.

Then Byron dropped the broken bottle to the floor.

"Git outta here!" Sally crowed at him.

Byron just looked at her, his eyes spinning like slot machines. He slowly turned and shuffled toward the door and tottered out into the night.

Don't never come back!" Sally wasn't done. "Ye hear me?!"

Pen looked at each pale face in the room. He stepped away from the corner and took his black leather jacket off the back of a chair and slipped into it. He wiped the blood dripping from his lower lip and picked up a full bottle of beer. Swallowed. Then he set the bottle down and grabbed hold of Byron's coat and he strolled out of the tavern without paying his tab.

21

THOUGH THE DRIVE BACK TO JOE'S was more slowed and calculated compared to the reckless hellride into town, Pen's drunkenness had nearly soared them off into the void while taking a wide curve on Highway 21. He later lost control on the gravel road to the farm and fishtailed the backend of the car into a row of tree roots lined above the ditch. Then when he pulled the black beauty up to the cabin and killed the engine, Byron's head fell over from his neck and he barfed up his booze and supper of pork and beans all over the floorboard.

"Fuck, man!" Pen shoved Byron in the shoulder. He felt the temptation to wallop him with a tire iron.

Byron's head lolled and his eyes rolled.

Pen heaved his frustration and hopped out. He went around to the passenger side and opened the door.

"We're home. Come on."

Byron didn't obey.

"By. Get your ass up."

Still no response.

"Fuck." Pen heaved. He seized Byron underneath an armpit to haul him up. "Come on, man."

"Fuck off me," Byron moaned, slinging his arm and socking Pen in the chest.

"Well fuck you then!" Pen howled. "Get your own drunk ass out!"

Byron roused and stuck his boots out to the ground one at a time. He struggled to heft his rear out from the low-riding seat. He looked like an upside-down crab escaping from its shell.

Pen noticed the wet spot soaking at Byron's crotch.

"Are you fuckin' serious?!"

Byron gave no reply to his pants-pissing performance.

Pen seethed and slammed the car door shut. Then they both staggered toward the cabin door, heads down and hushed, like a bickering married couple back home from a rained-out picnic.

Once inside, Byron headed straight for the bathroom, bouncing in-between the walls of the hallway. Pen halted in the kitchen and shook his head with spite.

"Crazy fuck."

He turned to the sink and reached for a pan on the countertop and let it fill up with faucet water and bubbly dishwashing soap. He then roamed the cabin in search of cleaning rags, and when he came across the muslin grain sack filled with hunting clothes that Byron had left laying by the fireplace, he figured something in it would do the trick.

He went back outside with the pan of soapy water and the grain sack in tow. When he opened the Firebird's passenger door, the rancid stink of urine and vomit emitted from inside. He winced, cussing Byron's name, then yanked a hunting vest out of the grain sack and went to scrubbing on his knees.

The fetid odor triggered his gullet to gag, and he turned to cussing himself for instigating the nightmare night. He told himself that he should've known Byron was too crazy to take to town. Too crazy to take anywhere. Hell, too crazy to stay anywhere. He then brought to mind how volatile Byron had turned at The Hoghead, and he imagined how his old buddy probably inflicted the same brand of violence upon Tara. How he'd hit her. How he'd kicked her. How he'd choked the living shit out of her. And the more he imagined, the hotter his temper rose, until he jerked up from his knees and angrily chucked the foul vest into the frosted yard and stomped back into the cabin with a glaring intent to speak his mind.

He rushed past the kitchen and into the living room and found the startling sight of Byron fully naked and hunched over a freshly sparked fire. "Next time you pull a bottle on me, mother fucker, you better goddamn use it!"

Byron said nothing. His head bowed to the fire.

"You almost strangled that son of a bitch to death, and for what? Cause he stole your goddamn beer?"

Byron did not move from his squat and did not return a word.

"Beatin' on people make you feel big or somethin'? That the way you treated Tara? Throttle her if you didn't like somethin' she done?"

Byron bolted up. His crystal gray eyes signaled that his wits were still drowning in a whirlpool of liquor.

"You don't know me!"

"I know goddamn enough!"

The two remained poised to rip one another apart, with the Aztec death mask peering down at them as witness.

"I didn't ask you here."

"Yeah, but you never was one for askin' were you?"

The two remained set to strike.

Daring who would hit first.

"She's as dead to me as the rest of it," Byron broke.

Then he turned and headed into the darkness of the hallway.

And vanished.

Pen stood rigid. Cautious. Watching the dark hallway. He couldn't snuff the thought that the unpredictable lunatic might come back with the thirty-ought Winchester.

After a couple of tense minutes, he slow-walked backward to hearth and took the firewood hatchet in his hand. He held it and stepped to the calf-skin chair and eased down.

While he waited for Byron's possible return, he began to muse upon the notion of killing him. He questioned if he was capable. He'd once thought that he'd beaten his daddy to death, but that turned out to be fiction. And then he began to wonder why it was that every decision and every direction he'd taken in his life turned out to be an act of straddling over a new desperation that he never saw coming.

<h1 style="text-align:center">22</h1>

WHEN HE LEFT DOE RUN thirteen years ago in his '66 Chevy, the transmission fell out while climbing the Rockies. He spent three days of hard drinking in Denver, pawned the truck off for bottom dollar, then bought a bus ticket west, figuring to exile himself to a place like God might've sent Cain.

He arrived in Los Angeles with a suitcase of clothes. He wired for the ten grand that he'd planned to spend on his elopement with Tara and wasted no time on blowing it on the pain-numbing powers of cocaine. And after a hedonistic month of sharing himself and his party favors with gorgeous gals who liked to ball with a devilish charmer, his ten grand ran dry.

A stretch of menial jobs followed. Tending bar. Cleaning pools. Driving cabs. Cutting lawns. Before he knew it, five fast forgettable years of living in the big, bad beautiful city had passed him by.

Then came the fateful night when he met a trio of sorority honeys at a UCLA bar. They said they were aching for a riotous time away from the schoolbooks and frat boys. After many rounds of tequila on his own dime, he drunkenly persuaded the honeys to tag along for a midnight ride to the beach, which then turned into a dare to break inside a Malibu country club for a skinny dip in its Olympic-size pool.

At five in the morning the Malibu cops arrived and hauled the naked foursome out of the water. He joked that it was only a little country-style fun, but the coppers weren't laughing at the two eight-balls of Columbian in his jeans. Neither were they sympathetic when he denied knowing that the three coked-up and drunk honeys were only nineteen.

Johnny Law's rap for his funny fiasco landed him a short stretch at the county jail. A few lonely days in a dark and dirty cell, beating the shakes and delusions, was all it took for him to swear off cocaine for good. Then six months later, on the day of his release, he got the hell out of California.

He drifted eastward. Another shitty job and another loose woman in each town. He then moved on to the next without reason.

Flagstaff. Albuquerque. Dallas. Houston. New Orleans. Tampa. Miami. Then in the fall of '89 he found himself standing on the island shore of Loggerhead Key. He was done with running. Tired of being broke. Tired of living alone. So he bought an Amtrak ticket and hopped the rails to the one place he figured he could bet his destiny solely with his will.

The moment he stepped onto the Vegas sidewalks he found the city uninviting for those with no cash. Three solid months he searched for work suitable toward his talents, tapping on the iron-barred doors of every loan shark in town, but not even one high dandy roller or one street curb scum would see him. With such disheartening prospects, he spent most of his broke days watching old ladies pull slot arms, and most of his miserable nights in seedy dives, biding his time until luck showed its shiny face. And it was on one of those routine nights of embittered boredom at a place called The Duck Inn that his luck walked through the door.

He was sitting on his regular barstool, minding his own business, when a burly Russian punk bounced inside. The punk strode up and accosted the bartender about the whereabouts of a deadbeat gambler who'd not paid up on a personal loan. The bartender got panicky and motioned his chin toward the backroom where the deadbeat was shooting pool.

The punk snorted. Then the punk strode in that direction. Along the way the punk picked up a pool stick from the wall rack and proceeded to raise it high and bring down upon the deadbeat's spine.

When the deadbeat moaned and claimed that he was busted, the punk split open a butterfly blade and slashed a nasty mark across the deadbeat's cheek.

As the other patrons of The Duck Inn scattered from the fray, he calmly left his barstool and walked to the backroom to stake his future. With no hesitation, he told the punk that he'd seen the deadbeat paying for a round of Crown Royals, and he suggested that the punk check the deadbeat's shoe.

The punk snarled in question. But the punk went ahead and hurled the deadbeat to the floor and yanked off the dead-beat's fake snakeskin loafer. A wad of twenties tumbled out.

It was a few months later when he was introduced to the Russian punk's Uncle Vik at a mansion in the desert. Over aged wine and bites of caviar, he learned that the Russian family had recently arrived in Vegas to expand their inter-ests. Though Uncle Vik was new to the loan shark trade, Uncle Vik knew that in desperate times people were more apt to take risky chances to gain money, and with the economy in the shitter Uncle Vik was more than willing to lend gambling funds to any poor sucker for a high interest profit in return.

Uncle Vik admitted to not usually hiring outside the bloodline. However, since his nephew vouched such a rousing recommendation, he was offered a job as a low-level collector.

The gig was simple. Track down deadbeats who were late on their loans and claim any valuables they had. And there were only three requirements for the job.

One: Obey instructions.

Two: No personal gambling.

Three: No skimming from collections.

If any of these requirements were broken, for any reason at all, there would not be a chance for redemption.

He was undecided on taking the offer at first, concerned that he might be selling whatever good might be left in him. But after considering that his other options were down to nil, he went ahead and shook hands with Uncle Vik and joined in.

The punk was assigned to show him the ropes, and so he had to stomach the broken legs, the gouged eyes, the pried-off teeth, and the cut-up faces that the punk happily bestowed upon the deadbeats they found. Then after a few months on the Petrov payroll, he'd gained enough trust that he was ordered to hit the road and hunt down the deadbeats who'd skipped Vegas for better luck at low-class casinos in Reno and Tahoe and Indian Lands.

Carrying the experience from his days as a repo-man, he possessed a wolf's instinct for the job. He nearly always found his prey. Sweating over cards. Crying over craps.

Raging over roulette wheels. And he could always pry a dollar or two from them by simply voicing his threats or delivering a strong fist belt to the gut. Never once did he have to go so far as to break bones or gash skin.

And so for three years he stayed satisfied with his gig with the Russians. Rarely did he glimpse toward another future. Besides the steady working days and working nights, he would sometimes bed a barmaid, or he would go drinking with the punk and old-school Russian clan. He would sit quietly and listen to them reminisce about their golden days of lawbreaking, when they'd held up jewelry shops and small banks, long before the drug-running whackos tainted the criminal trade. All in all, he considered Vegas to be the perfect set-up. No reason to leave. No better place to go. But then came another fateful night when the punk requested for him to partner up and come along for a special late-night collection.

They rode together across town in the punk's black Mercedes and arrived at the sleazy motel where the chosen deadbeat was known to be staying. The punk forked over twenty bucks to the scared Bangladeshi motel manager to borrow the master key, and when they stormed into the room, they found the deadbeat with his pants down and a Chinese hooker blowing him.

The punk laughed and started kicking the deadbeat in the groin, slugging his face, while the Chinese hooker screamed and ran and escaped into the bathroom.

He stood back and watched. Wishing he was somewhere else.

The deadbeat keeled over with clots of blood flowing over his chin and chest. The punk turned around with a sick grin, asking him if he wanted to take a couple of free swings, and it was enough pause for the deadbeat to charge for the hidden snub-nose .38 stuffed under a pillow.

The gun thundered.

The bullet found the punk's shoulder.

The punk jerked but recovered. Then the punk whipped out his butterfly blade and began jabbing the deadbeat's neck, sending a shower of blood upon the wall.

The deadbeat stopped moving. A stream of blood gurgled at the deadbeat's throat. The punk leaned down and picked up the .38 snub nose from the floor and marched to the bathroom door. The punk kicked it open and shot four bullets into the screaming Chinese hooker.

And then he and punk ran out of the motel room.

Both of their names now christened as killers.

ONE DAY UNTIL
DEER SEASON

23

TARA HAD TOSSED AND TURNED all night underneath the patch-work quilt that her maternal grandmother had given to her as a wedding gift. It was now 7:45 in the morning and she was sleepily awake in bed.

As her head flopped over on the goose-down pillow, her eyes met the rays of the sun peeking through the window curtains. She wanted to believe it was God appearing in His glorious splendor. She held her breath and listened for His words of wisdom.

But God didn't speak.

Feeling vanquished by His unceasing silence, her eyes mournfully fell away from the light and followed up the wall to hit upon a framed photograph of the boy. It was his third-grade school picture. The sole memento of him that she'd kept out of the storage boxes packed away inside a church member's garage. It had been hanging there since she'd moved in with the preacher and his wife, yet sadly it had become little more than an overlooked decoration for the uninspiring room. As she now studied the boy's face, it brought to mind how she used to scrutinize his lips and cheeks and brow when he was alive. How she used to probe him for subtle features of his father.

Feeling the guilt and shame she kept locked inside herself, she averted her eyes from the boy's picture, and tried to force her mind into believing that her marriage to Byron and her motherhood had not been shams, even though they had both begun and ended in rumored scandals.

Yes, she reminded herself, in the beginning there had been those town gossips about how the decent daughter of the elementary school teachers had gotten herself indecently impregnated by the shy young man called Spook. And yes, there had been the other rumors of how she and Byron had pleased her displeased decent folks with a hasty elopement at Eureka Springs. But all that rumor talk went away, didn't it? Folks had come to like Byron once they got to know him. They'd seen that he was a normal man, no different than most. And their marriage had become like any other, at least up until. . .

Her eyes fell toward the light again, waiting for God to say anything at all. Again, He said nothing. So in an attempt to con her guilty self further, her mind began to run through the clustered memories of how affectionate Byron had been to a child he never knew was not his.

She remembered how Byron had burped the boy's back with his bearlike hands, how he'd rocked the boy to sleep on stormy nights. How he'd spoon fed the boy's gummy mouth, how he'd whistled while changing the boy's diapers. How he'd shown the boy the way to hit a baseball, how to pedal a bicycle, how to fish for perch with a cane rod. She remembered how during the summertime Byron and the boy would go to afternoon rodeos and nighttime carnivals, and on all-day canoe floats on muddy rivers, and on morning walks through the colorful forests to see the mysterious wonders of the woods. She remembered how Byron had loved the boy more than he loved her, and how she had grown to love Byron because of it.

Then she tried to forget it all.

She tried to forget the hot July night two summers ago when the sheriff had awakened her and Byron with the woeful tale that the miracle child was dead. She tried to forget how Byron began to hate the world and how he lost his sanity in the murk of liquor. She tried to forget how their marriage went with the boy's coffin, buried deep inside the cold dark earth to never come back again.

The rapid run of dead memories was bringing her to tears, and so she tossed the warm quilt from her body and rose up off the bed to try and shake away the old pains. She grabbed her terry cloth robe from the floor and hugged the sleeves over her shoulders. Then she opened the bedroom door to walk out into the world and face whatever lingering tragedies the day might bring.

The preacher was comfortably parked into his recliner in the living room, devotedly studying the second book of Samuel. When Tara's bedroom door cracked open, he turned around in his seat and saw her coming toward him. His first thought was that she looked like a sickly pale scarecrow in need of fresh straw.

"Mornin' Tara. Not feelin' well?"

"I wasn't up for workin' today is all."

She sniffed and rubbed her nose. She took a seat on the sofa and put her feet underneath her. She sniffed again.

The holy man sensed she needed to unburden a sorrow off her chest. He dog-eared the page that told how Absalom ordered the death of his brother Amnon for the abomination of defiling their sister.

"That's him, huh?"

She fought to form a smile.

"Yes, that's him."

"Seems nice enough."

She bit her lower lip and played with her fingers.

"What do you think I should do?"

"What about?"

"Should I tell him?"

Her eyes begged for him to choose the answer for her.

"You mean about Jake?"

She nodded. "Yes."

The preacher rubbed his fingers over his mouth, measuring a notion in his head.

"Tara. . ."

He exhaled his thought to make room for an improved one.

"You're askin' me somethin' I'm not sure I have a good answer for."

"I'm just so sick of livin' these secrets." She wiped a tear from her eye. "It almost ain't worth livin' at all."

"Hey now."

The preacher scooted on the edge of the recliner and reached a sympathetic hand out to comfort hers.

"Don't you go thinkin' like that. You've given yourself to God. That's worth all this life has to offer."

"Then why do I feel like such a horrible person?"

Both of her eyes squeezed thick tears.

The preacher puckered his lips in contemplation.

"I know sometimes things can get awful confusin'. But we have to hold faith. You have to forgive yourself. Know that you're doin' right in His eyes."

"I've been holdin' faith!"

She swallowed the balloon expanding in her throat.

"And nothin's changed. Nothin's changed."

The preacher let loose of her hand and let her cry. He knew that if he had a better answer for her then it was bungled somewhere inside his aged mind.

"You've done nothin' wrong, Tara. Seein' this fella has just got you rememberin' old wounds is all. But you haven't done anything wrong. God hasn't left you. He's still here."

Her wet eyes were still pleading for the answer. "What am I supposed to do?"

He stared blankly across the room, feeling like a blind and deaf idiot to the knowledge of the Almighty.

"I try my best to believe His truth, Tara. That's all any of us can do." His affecting eyes gazed back upon her. "But I fear that a lot more hurt might come if you tell that man he fathered a son that he'll never be able to know or see. And I don't even wanna think what Byron might do if he caught wind of it. We both know what he's capable of doin'."

Tara said nothing. But her bowed head and silence said enough.

The preacher exhaled and wiped the side of his lips with the tips of his fingers again, considering all things in a holy manner as a preacher does.

"As far as what God wants you to do. . . I don't rightly know, Tara. I just don't rightly know."

24

PEN HEARD A FAINT POW GO OFF in his ears. His lids popped open and blinked his dry eyes. He could taste the iron of blood inside his raw and tender cheek.

Pow.

He heard it again. Distant and barely there. He let out a pained groan, wondering where he'd been this time around. His forehead felt as if a stone sculptor had been carving his brain with a chisel and mallet.

He raised his stiff frame up from the couch to find his clothes and boots clung on. When he noticed the hatchet on the floor, the night's tales all came back to him in sequence.

The joints.

The Hoghead.

Jim Beam and Budweiser.

The cheerleaders.

One-ear.

And vomit.

Pow.

He rubbed his sore temples and twisted around toward

the window. He pulled back the curtains and the harsh sunlight scorched straight through his pupils.

"Jesus."

His face puckered and his eyelids squeezed to avoid another blinding punch as he squinted out to the field. No visible signs of the sound. Yet he was well-acquainted with the report of a rifle.

Pow.

He let go of the curtain and dabbed the inside of swollen cheek with his middle finger. He ran his hand over his face and wiped the oily grease that had seeped through his pores. He glanced over the room and breathed the stale air that reeked of fireplace ash. And he knew right then that he could no longer stay with the out-of-control maniac who resided here.

Pow.

He leaned over and stretched toward the end of the couch and grabbed his duffle bag. He placed it between his boots and unzipped it then reached inside to retrieve the Colt. He gripped the pistol sturdily in his hand. His head twisted toward the window again. It was a sunny morning alright. An ideal time to face the music and say so long to his old friend.

Byron was crouched in a shooting position, his elbows resting on his raised knees, his hands gripping the thirty-ought at its stock and trigger. His head was jutted forward from his neck and his right eye was pasted firmly to the Redfield scope.

Two hundred yards away, an ivory white horse skull was hung up onto the trunk of a sycamore tree. It had eight holes plugged through its forehead, and when the Winchester fired a bullet for the ninth one, the sound erupted over the entire valley of the farm.

Pow.

The bolt action of the thirty-ought released and sent the brass casing flying out from the smoking chamber. It landed in the vicinity of the eight others cooling on the soggy grass.

Byron took a relaxed breath and spat with satisfaction of his aim. His head then swiveled around to see Pen soft-stepping toward him through the mushy ground. And dangling from his hand was what looked to be a pistol.

As Pen drew closer, Byron rose from his squatted position. The rifle barrel angled in front of him. When the two met and stood face to face, no greetings were exchanged. Only silent shared reminders of their mutual likes and dislikes for one another. Then Pen flipped the Colt like an Annie Oakley trick and caught it by its barrel.

"Thought you might like to swap some shots."

Byron delayed a trade of weapons, but then lowered the Winchester from his chest and held it out so Pen could safely step forward and seize it by its stock.

"There's one in the chamber," he muttered, while his other hand reached and snatched the Colt.

Pen felt the length of the rifle, admiring it. He stuck the butt to his shoulder and peered through the scope.

"What are you shootin' at?"

Byron pointed with the Colt.

"That skull hung up in those line of trees yonder."

"Ain't you got somethin' not already dead?"

They both narrowed their eyes and craned their heads in search of a breathing target. Byron was the first to spot two mourning doves fluttering across the sky, and without hesitation, he swung the Colt up and fired all eight rounds before Pen was even aware that there were birds in the air.

"Fuck man," Pen snapped. "It ain't a goddamn Gatlin' gun."

Byron measured the weight of the .45 in his hand. Pen shook his head, annoyed that his kill toy had been treated so rudely. He whipped the Winchester back to his shoulder and aimed at the horse skull. The kaboom rang in his ears as soon as he squeezed the trigger. He ejected the spent shell and fired again. And again.

"Not much kick."

They swapped their weapons back and fondled them like two spoiled brats happy to have their favorite playthings in their own hands again. Neither man could conjure a word to say to the other.

Byron bent down to pick up the spent shells out of the wet grass. Pen slid the empty clip out of the Colt's butt and put it in his jacket pocket then kneeled to retrieve the .45 casings.

"You remember that time we were jumpin' off the Little Sugar Creek bridge, and I almost drown?"

"I remember pullin' your ass to the bank. You almost took me down with you."

"That's what I get for chuggin' a fifth of peach schnapps then tryin' to swim with my boots on."

Pen blew into an empty casing, sounding a low whistle.

"You know how some people who nearly die, but don't, say they seen their whole life flash right before their eyes when it happened? How they saw a light or a tunnel or some shit? I don't think I ever told anybody this, but somethin' like that happened to me in that river that day. Believe me?"

"I ain't got no real thought on it."

Pen formed a smile that wasn't a smile. They both came to their feet, coolly studying the bullet shells in their palms.

Pen's eyes fell away into the horizon, searching for some grand purpose.

"Hell, I's probably just drunk. Lookin' up to the sunlight from underneath the water and my sight just playin' tricks on me. What was weird about it though, I didn't see my life flash by like people say it does. I saw everybody else. My mom. The old man. I even seen you. I could hear and see all of you together. Kind of like when you see tadpoles get stuck at the top of a frozen pond, you know? That's what dyin' was like for me anyway."

Pen banged a second clip of bullets into the butt of Colt. Then his head came back around, and they held their hard stares at one another as the morning breeze whipped up around them.

"Try her again?"

"I've had enough."

"Yeah." Pen nodded. "Me too."

Then Pen turned his back and walked away in a cold silence, leaving his old buddy standing there alone in the field and cradling the unloaded Winchester in his arms like it was a thin sleeping child.

<h1 style="text-align:center">25</h1>

PEN DIDN'T TAKE MUCH TIME to tidy up, other than a splash in the sink and a clean shirt tossed on his back, before he was behind the wheel of the Firebird and climbing up the high hill slope. He gave the cabin a last look in the rearview and muttered, "*Adios* Joe," knowing that he'd never set foot on the place again. "Sorry I missed you."

Over the three-mile stretch of bumpy gravel, his head felt so awful that he couldn't bring himself to light a Camel, plus the stench of puke and dishwashing soap inside the car was making his stomach roll. Then when he met the asphalt of Highway 21 and turned westward toward Doe Run, the strong sunlight angrily hit him through the windshield.

He flipped the visor down and grabbed his aviator sunglasses inside the console and slipped them over his red meat eyes to battle the blinding rays. Then once he felt settled down for the rest of the drive into town, he switched hands on the wheel and held the speed below the limit and prayed the day wouldn't bring him too many more aggravations.

Along the winding road, he was met by a convoy of buck

hunters in their camper trucks and vans. Passing by with their eager grins on their hairy mugs and orange hats donned on their heads and rifles racked in their back windows. He reckoned the whole countryside had gone bloodthirsty mad.

It was near eleven o'clock when he pulled into the Town & County Bank parking lot. It was full save for one space, and so he eased the Firebird into it and cut the engine. He slid the sunglasses down the bridge of his nose and checked his appearance in the rearview. He determined that he looked like a cold plate of dogshit and he questioned himself why he'd come.

Maybe the bank had made a mistake. Maybe he could summon the ghost of his dead rotten daddy and charm Butt Burns for a loan. Maybe he was just so damn desperate for some money that he hoped the Good Lord would provide.

When he opened the door and got out of the car, he noticed the grain sack of hunting garb still tucked away in the backseat. He thought about shoving an orange cap on his greasy-hair head to look a little more presentable, but then the idea seemed idiotic to him.

He shut the door and strolled across the parking lot, tapping his fist at the heartburn erupting inside his guts.

As he waltzed into the bank lobby, wearing his dark shades and mean glare behind them, he saw the four lines to the teller windows were eight heads deep. A general lot of muddy farmhands, harping housewives, hurried store owners, filthy loggers and millers, poor-ass welfare beggars, blue-haired retirees, and a couple of ugly beauty shop gals. Not desiring to waste his time wading through the crowd, he beelined for Burns' chunky secretary. She was busy typing a loan agreement and he shook her up a little when came up behind her and grumbled something that sounded like good morning.

"Can I help you?"

"I'm here to see Teddy Burns," he answered directly. His usual charm squashed by a foul mood and aching head.

"Mr. Cullen, right?" she inquired, tossing her batty eyes. "You were here a couple days ago?"

"Yeah. Teddy told me to come for some papers."

"Let me check."

She picked up the phone and punched a button.

Through his sunglasses he peeped down her blouse and saw a white lacy bra and pair of flesh pillows. He wished he could lay his hammering head down on them for a nap.

"Mr. Burns? Mr. Cullen is here to see you," she told the phone. "Okay, I'll let him know." She hung up and peered at him. "He'll be right out."

Pen nodded at her without smiling. "Dandy."

"My pleasure," she acknowledged, and went back to typing.

He wandered leisurely in the direction of Burns' office, his shaded eyes shifting over the lobby and to the extended lines of customers. The four fat old tellers were shoveling out cash like it was corn cobs into a pig trough.

He then glanced up at the steel gun turret hovering over the lobby like a cycloptic iron eyeball, and he imagined how Bonny and Clyde must've given them old-time bank bastards one scary shit in the pants back in the day.

The office door swung open and out came Burns with his stupid banker's grin stretched wide.

"Mornin' Pen. How you doin'?"

Pen nodded. "Mornin' Teddy."

"Come on in."

Pen shuffled his way past Burns and into the office. A tall and gangly red-haired man with a bushy mustache and thick glasses was sitting in a corner chair, looking over a handful of papers. He was wearing camo pants and a camo button-up shirt and a camo hat. Pen thought he looked like a hedge growing in the room.

"Hello," said the man, bobbing his red-haired head, barely taking his attention off from his reading.

"This here is Frank Carter, the bank's attorney," Burns introduced him. "He's brought the estate agreements."

"Ted was telling me of your expertise in repoing," the lawyer spoke up, cordially and friendly-like. "That's quite a story."

"Yeah, well I got a few." Pen sniffed, not caring to be friendly. "You got somethin' I need to sign?"

"Oh, no. Nothin' legal anyway," Burns assured, waving his hand. "Just gotta give you the agreements we had with your dad is all." He moved to the edge of his desk to pilfer through a stack of legal papers. "I got 'em in here somewhere."

"You taking in any hunting?" Carter asked.

Pen shook his head. "Not really my thing."

"On my way to meet my son in the woods right after I leave here," Carter felt obliged to say. "I have a sixty-acre farm over near West Plains with a good patch of woods on it. We still like to carry on the tradition, don't really care if we get a deer or not."

"Here we are." Burns had found the right papers and he reached over the desk to hand them to Pen.

Pen fanned the stack with his thumb. "This it?"

"That's it," Burns confirmed.

"Where'd you bag them bucks, Ted?" Carter asked, nudging his chin toward the mounted deer heads on the wall.

Burns forced an uncomfortable laugh. "Aw, I bought 'em cheap at an auction. Huntin's not really my thing either."

Carter smirked, unimpressed, and went back to reading.

"Besides, I gotta work in the mornin'," Burns added, trying to save his reputation. "Oh shoot, I almost forgot." He reached for the stack of papers from Pen's hands. "May I see those again right quick? Just the back few."

Pen offered the last ten pages of the stack, and Burns scanned a couple. "When we was closin' out your dad's accounts we came across one of yours," the banker revealed.

"One of mine?"

"Yeah, a savings account." Burns located the right record. "Here it is. The date says it was opened all the way back in sixty-eight."

Pen grabbed the paper and glanced at the name Mary Cullen typed at the top. He guessed that she must've started a piggy bank for him back when she first began working as a teller.

"Looks like it's gained quite a bit of interest since then, huh?" Burns amusingly voiced, etching his stupid banker's grin.

When Pen's sight reached the bottom, he saw the account was currently holding a not-so-staggering amount of two hundred and twenty-six dollars and twenty-seven cents. It was all he could muster to fight his urge to knock that stupid banker's grin off the stupid banker's face.

26

PEN COOLLY TRACKED OUT OF THE BANK and headed to the Firebird. Once he got behind the wheel, he immediately cranked the ignition and threw the gearshift into drive and got the hell out of the parking lot. He drove straight to Jessup's gas station for a fill-up. He hopped out quick, gripped the handle of the pump and flipped it on, then he twisted the cap off the tank and shoved the handle of the pump into the hole and squeezed. It wasn't until then that he felt himself take a breath since walking out of Butt Burns' office.

Deep down he knew that he should be tickled pink that he had a little cash to gas up and leave town now, yet waves of woe were washing inside of him. The instant he had glimpsed his mother's name on that savings account, his hardened emotions had fallen back to those of the blameless boy who had watched her die, and he was feeling an urge to cry.

"What say?"

He spun around to see yellow-teeth Wayne strolling out of the station door, working a rag with his greasy fingers.

When he spotted the fresh scratches on the Firebird's paint his whole face dropped in despair.

"Shit man." He ran his fingertips across the scratches on the Firebird's metal. "That's a cryin' shame right there."

Pen looked away, not desiring to elaborate on the mundane details of sliding into the ditch last night.

"I got the money I owe you."

"I trusted you would." Wayne hawked up snot and spat it on the concrete. "You kiss another deer or somethin'?"

Pen set the pump handle to lock so it'd pour on its own.

"I gotta go hit the john."

And he coldly walked away.

Wayne felt the obvious brush off.

"Well fuck you too, bud," he whispered out of earshot.

Pen cut straight into the gas station, past the counter, into the men's restroom. But even as he relieved himself into the stool, he still couldn't shake the memory of his dead mom. His throat started growing a rock and a strange sense of duty hit him to thank her. He then zipped up and washed off and walked out of the pisser with slightly less agitation toward the day.

Wayne was waiting at the register. His yellow-teeth not smiling anymore. Pen grabbed a glazed bearclaw and a cup of stalwart black coffee to jolt his sleeping senses awake and placed them on the counter.

"Okay. Let's see." Wayne was strictly business, punching numbers on the register with his greasy forefinger. "Fifty for the tow. Gas was twenty-two twenty-nine on the first fill-up. For this one it's nineteen sixty-eight. Fifty-five cents for the bear claw with tax. And a quarter for the coffee. All in, looks to be ninety-two dollars and seventy-seven cents."

Pen placed five twenties on the counter. He stared at the

crispness of the Jacksons, considering that he was leaving town with little more than he'd come with.

"Appreciate the local rate on the tow." He said it sincerely. "You didn't have to do that."

Wayne pinched the bills and licked his grimy thumb to count them and placed them into the register slots.

"You find Byron Tisdale?"

Pen looked away from the greasy gas man toward the Busch beer clock. "Sure didn't." It was pushing noon.

Wayne smirked and counted out the change onto the counter.

Pen clutched the crumpled five and ones, and said, "Thanks again," then turned and strode out with nothing more to say.

Once he was back behind the wheel of the Firebird, he turned the key and checked the fuel gauge. Full tank. He blew a big breath of relief over knowing that he could hit the highway and be done with this goddamn town. Just one last thing to do.

A couple miles out TT Highway he arrived at the cemetery. He pulled into the driveway and crept past the tall lime-stone columns to enter the haunting grounds. Only a few vacancies were left for the living, and judging by the number of erected tombstones, he concluded that a whole lot of old-timers were now fertilizing the grass since the last time he'd been here.

He parked the Firebird beside a dogwood tree where two cardinals darted upon its stick branches. When the engine died down the creepy tranquility of the death yard nearly suffocated him, and a sudden inspiration to leave entered his mind. But he felt obligated to evince his gratitude to his dead mom, plus he wanted to see for certain that his rotten daddy was underground.

He stepped out of the car and lit his first Camel of the day. He then followed the chat road that cut through the rows of gravestones, his eyes marking the names of the dead. Davis. Henderson. Robertson. Able. Berens. Probsfield. Campbell. Raley. Names he'd heard of, names he hadn't. Flat headstones. Others in the shape of a cross. One looked like a white tree with *Woodsmen of the World* carved into its marble bark. Another had a stone baby angel with tiny wings spread in flight.

He came near his family's resting place and stepped from the chat path onto the brown lawn growing over the corpses. At the end of the line he came to two modest grave markers made of gray granite.

Mary Anne Cullen
Born September 2, 1946
Died March 15, 1971

Greg Lee Cullen
Born July 29, 1932
Died March 12, 1993

With such scant written history, he could not help but realize how foreign all three of them were to one another. Husband. Wife. Mother. Father. Son. Meaningless tags clamped onto them by the world's blind misunderstandings.

As he stared at his mother's name he remembered when she had shown him a dozen or so faded family photographs that she'd kept stored in a torn shoebox. She had told him of how they were descendants from no-good relations from some Kentucky town, and she had said that his daddy had worked there at the coal mines. She had said that his daddy was nearing his thirties when he first took up with her, even though she was only a green fourteen at the time and had never been with a man. She had alleged that their hasty marriage had ignited a bad feud between their blood kin, and so they had to hightail it out of Kentucky with little more than the clothes on their backs and a '56 Ford Mercury. She had claimed they were headed westward to California, but his daddy halted and stayed in Missouri after learning that a local lead mine was paying good wages to experienced miners.

That was in '61.

And he, their sole offspring, was born a year after.

He then remembered how his daddy had worked at that lead mine for six solid years until his spinal injury--or self-claimed spinal injury--and how his daddy had won the two hundred grand insurance settlement. He remembered how his daddy had hoarded his riches and only thrifted on himself and how his poor mother had to take on the role of family provider, working at the bank, until she came down with cancer and passed away in '71.

He glared at his daddy's head stone and spit. He then glanced over to a neighboring gravestone of a dead man named James Ellington, and laying atop it was an arrangement of fading chrysanthemums and baby's breath.

He stepped toward it and took the flora in his hand and brought them to his nostrils for a whiff. They smelled a perfume of pale sweetness and decay.

He crossed back to his family's graves and began to pick off the petals one by one, letting them float like snowflakes over his mother's petty stone. He sought to find the proper words to say as wetness shaped in the corners of his eyes. He wiped the tears with the heel of his hand and tried to strengthen his fickle nerves to speak. After a couple minutes of dull silence, he realized that there were no words to express the chasm of hollowness inside of him. And so he scuttled away with no spoken or whispered goodbye to the dead strangers who had raised him.

When he neared back to the Firebird, his sight again caught upon the monument with the stone baby angel, and this time he spotted the carved name and an oval portrait of the deceased.

Jacob Henry Tisdale
Born February 7, 1981
Died July 9, 1991
A life of a boy. A lifetime of love.

He crept closer to the monument and peered into the beaming face of the little boy staring back at him. The child's rounded face was the same shape as Tara's. The skin ivory with faintly spotted freckles. The eyes cinnamon. The hair shiny light brown. Yet the child's face also held a strange familiarity that he had peered at in mirrors.

He noted the child's birth date.

He calculated time in his head.

And then he knew.

27

SINCE EARLY MORNING, Tara had been tidying up the church to atone for yesterday's carnal sin. So far, she had praised God by vacuuming the ragged red carpet and wiping down the twenty rows of varnished pine pews and mending the torn songbooks with tape and glue. She was now hunched down inside the sanctified realm of the preacher's pulpit, vigorously polishing the dusty feet of a plastic Christ and the rugged plastic cross he was spiked upon.

"If I didn't know any better," a voice boomed throughout the hollow room, "I'd say you was the Virgin Mary."

She rose and spun around.

Pen stood in the back entranceway.

"You scared me," she reacted in a strained breath.

"The preacher's wife next-door said you's here."

She smiled. Too stunned to do anything else. And watched him begin a slow stroll down the aisle like a sinner coming toward her to repent.

With each step his fingers drummed over the tops of the pews while his wandering eyes rolled to appraise the holy space. The water-stained ceiling. The colored-glass windows. The crookedly hung bulletin board showing last Sunday's attendance of sixty-eight God-fearing souls and their humble offering of $458.39. When he reached the end of the path, he stopped in front of a pinewood table with a communion serving tray set on top.

"Not exactly a cathedral, is it?"

"Not quite," Tara replied, half-smiling. She was glad to see him. Yet she was also too terrified to step away from the crucified Christ hovering over her. She embarrassingly wiped her dirty hands on her pants and set a can of furniture polish and a soiled sock on the preacher's podium.

He lifted off the metal top of the communion tray and picked out a one-swallow clear cup from its hole.

"Real wine or grape juice?"

"Grape juice."

"Too bad." He examined the emptiness of the one-swallow cup. "Might get more saved souls comin' on Sunday mornings if it was the real deal."

"Well, that might not be the best reason to come to church," she replied, this time with an honest smile.

He inserted the empty drinking cup back into the tray.

"I wanted to come by and say so long before I took off this time."

"Oh." There was a sting in her sound that matched the hurt in her face. "So, you got everythin' settled then?"

"Not quite everything."

He placed the metal top back onto the communion tray.

"I just went out to the graveyard to see the dead relations. A headstone don't say a whole lot about a life, does it?"

His eyes met hers and they stared into one another.

"Was the kid mine?"

Her face went grim.

"Was he?"

Then her eyes fell into despair.

"Was the kid mine?" he asked again.

"I, I didn't know how. . ."

Though she wanted to say it, the thirteen-year-old secret would not release from her held breath.

"Just tell me!"

"You left."

His glare at her went black and belligerent.

"I wanted you to know. . ." she tried again. "More than anything, I wanted you to know."

"So he was?!"

Her face squeezed and her head bobbed up and down.

He stiffened. Stopped breathing. Took his eyes away from her and the truth of it. Then his arm snapped up like a bull-whip and sent the communion tray flying across the pulpit.

"Please!" she screamed, dropping behind the table and covering her head with her arms in supplication.

When he looked back upon her, part of him wanted to reach out and comfort her, but most of him wanted to rip out the dirty guile within her.

"What the fuck did I ever see in you?"

He spun and marched in a fit of fury down the narrow aisle between the pews, knowing that if he remained there any longer then he would burn the whole damn church to the ground.

Tara remained cowered on the floor, reaching her hands out as if she possessed powers to pull him back.

"Pen. . . Wait. . . Wait!"

But he was already gone.

28

HE HAD THE FIREBIRD PEGGED at 90 mph as he screamed past the *On the Leading Edge of Progress* billboard.

He flew around a traffic line of traveling hunters and slow-poke farmers and families.

Past the carcass of the dead doe.

Past the crossroad where he'd tried to outrun the state smokey in his daddy's prized Mustang.

All the while his mind was racing to catch up with the many lies that had been living beyond him over the past thirteen years.

The last time he'd left Doe Run, he was running away from his daddy's meanness, and the shame inflicted on him by his girl and friend, and now here he was on the same road that had circled back to his fateful beginnings. This time, he was running away without his daddy's worth that he'd come to get, and instead, he was carrying the cruel truth of fathering a dead son.

On and on he drove, compelled to keep the gas at full throttle, daring himself to crash and burn into oblivion, wishing that he'd never come back, until he hit the Arkansas line and remembered that there was nowhere left for him to run.

Because the Bangladeshi motel manager could finger him and the Russian punk as the killers of the dead deadbeat and Chinese hooker, Uncle Vik had ordered them both to get out of Vegas.

While the punk nephew was ushered back to the mean streets of San Francisco, he was told to find his own dark corner of the world. He was given $5,000 and a Colt .45. Uncle Vik also vowed to keep an eye on his future well-being, financial and otherwise. And as a parting gift for his loyalty to the family, he was handed the keys to a black '75 Firebird Formula that the family kept stored in their stable of sweet rides. Though he'd not been the one who pulled the trigger, or even would've done so, all things considered, he knew it was more than a fair deal.

He headed south that night. When he hit Yuma at sunrise, he pulled the Firebird off the highway at a taco stand. While killing his hunger with a chorizo burrito, he studied the congregation of border-hoppers and cranky retirees and asshole yuppie artists, and the notion came to him that the transient town might be a decent enough hole to hide himself until the heat on him died down.

He stayed buried in Yuma for the next nine months. Living like a blind mole crawling underground. No women. No bars. Just a nightly six-pack of cold *cervezas* and a whole lot of down time. The blistering hot days of exile became mind-numbing. But he accepted that his outsider existence in the desert was far better than rotting away in Johnny Law's barred cage. Thankfully, Uncle Vik lived up to his word by twice sending a bundle of spending cash, delivered by one of the Russian goons. The goon also brought along his mail, as he had kept a Vegas post office box registered in his name in case some news of great magnitude from the world needed to reach him.

To keep his sanity from melting into soup, he pumped iron and ran six miles every day. He also rented a garage from a mute Cocopah Indian mechanic named Toad, and together they retooled the Firebird's motor with new plugs and valves, fuel lines and gaskets, all while smoking pipe bowls of dope the soundless Indian supplied.

Once the black beauty became lean and mean, he would sometimes take it out for midnight runs through the sleepy streets of Yuma. He would cruise past the old Territorial Prison and imagine the teeny dark cages that had once held murderous desperados and villains. He pictured them chained to the stone floor, cooking like raw meat in the summer sun. He weighed how most of those bad men had died there in misery. Then he would drive on, trying to forget about the prisoner ghosts, hoping he would not end up the same way.

On his last midnight run he took a deserted highway and punched the gas till the redline tacked all the way around to the bottom of the speedometer. As he sped beneath the blue-black sky, filled with its thousand flecks of starfire, he found himself screaming for mercy to the celestial heavens above. He screamed to Queen Cassiopeia and to the Chains of the Pleiades, then screamed to the Twin Bears and the Golden Belt of Orion, and when he ran out of stars that he knew the names of, he screamed to any supreme being that might exist to deliver him out of his purgatory.

When he again got down to his last few hundred dollars, he dialed up Uncle Vik from a pay phone to inquire when the next bag of cash was coming. One of the Russian goons answered the line and told him the grave news that had recently arrived from the mean streets of San Francisco. Apparently, the punk nephew had not cooled his hothead and a trio of Oakland bikers had lopped it off over a disputed ecstasy deal. The goon then relayed that because of the tragic loss, Uncle Vik was longer concerned with shielding the family's connection to the dead deadbeat and dead Chinese hooker, and so not another dime would be sent to him from Vegas.

He took the news as his death sentence. Then the goon offered another bit of news. A letter had arrived at the post office box in Vegas, and the embossed address on the envelope said it had come from the Town & County Bank in Doe Run. He permitted the goon to open the envelope and read the contents over the phone line. It was then that he learned the godsent news that his rotten daddy was truly dead. And there was mention of a family estate.

By mid-afternoon he was back in Doe Run. Cruising up and down Broadway. Fuming over the forces of his fate. Forging his will to change it.

He turned onto Central Avenue and went down until he was within eyeshot of the Town & County Bank.

He slowed and parked alongside the curb.

For the next half-hour he sat there behind the wheel. Counting how many cars and trucks pulled into the bank's lot. Counting how many customers came and went inside.

Though he had been ignoring its growth, the seed had

planted itself into his brain the moment Butt Burns had told him the bank was withholding the inheritance that he'd driven two thousand miles to claim. While listening to the sissy banker blab about the reasons why, he had imagined himself grabbing his Colt from his duffle bag and demanding the money anyway.

Of course, his wise sense had known then that such an impromptu act of armed robbery would've only landed him in the state penitentiary. Still, the dream of strolling into the bank with his .45 and demanding his family's nut hadn't completely drifted away. If anything, the dream had been swelling like a wildfire in the wind, and it blew into a blaze earlier this morning when he beheld all the deposit money pouring in from the booming deer season business. The only matter left was whether he was still sensible enough to douse those rising flames before they raged into an inferno and engulfed all the moral rectitude left in him.

After thirty more minutes of sitting alongside the curb, he crushed the butt of his third Camel into the ashtray and cranked up the engine. Then he wheeled away and drove past the bank, glimpsing it one last time to salt away in his memory.

He toured the narrow side streets of town. Some routes he traveled once. Others he retook no fewer than five times. Each neighborhood he made out how many vehicles sat in driveways. Which places had barking dogs. Noted where housewives were outside beautifying lawns. Which sidewalks folks were stretching their legs. Every street seemed to have roving eyes and he'd all but given up until he came upon a bright prospect at the dead-end of Euclid Way.

The sad slumped house looked to be vacant. A bent-tin real estate sign said it was for sale. He assumed if anybody did dwell inside then they'd have to be reclusive sons of bitches. Weeds grown a foot high. Unraked fallen leaves heaped against the front porch steps. Wrapped newspapers in the driveway. A rusted mailbox stuffed with junk mail. And thick brush growing wild in the backyard and beyond.

He braked the Firebird to a full stop. He surveyed the poor-quality houses next door and across the street. He didn't spy any nosey faces in the windows. Didn't see tricycles or swing sets or visible signs of kids who might play out-of-doors.

It certainly appeared to be a spot where someone could hide if a dicey situation got too hot. Best of all, the sad slumped house was only four short blocks from the Town & County Bank.

29

BYRON HADN'T ROLLED OUT OF BED before sunup this morning. Hadn't partaken of his breakfast of Ten High. Hadn't gone to Osage Bend. Yet all these changes had been deliberately planned for today. He didn't scout the woods because he didn't wish to inadvertently spook his trophy on the eve of the hunt. He also needed to be fairly sober to fire a dead-ly-aimed bullet tomorrow, so he was using today to wean himself off the liquor. And the nagging distraction of hav-ing Pen Cullen around had fatefully taken care of itself after his old friend drove away from the farm for good. He still couldn't piece together what all had happened between them last night, other than some disagreement over something or other. The scabs and cuts on his knuckles only told so much.

After he'd sighted the Winchester on the horse skull, he stayed inside the cabin and went about with the rest of his to-dos. He spent the remaining morning hours sitting on the calfskin chair beside the fire. Meticulously cleaning the thirty-ought. Concentrating on the hunt.

At half-past noon his fingers began to tremble. At one o'clock his whole hands quivered. Before two he was seeing shadows soar across the room. Soon he saw the shapes grow horns and knife-like claws.

At three, his little boy came to him. The child's face was blown away and maggots were squirming in the empty eye sockets. It was then that he decided to rush to the liquor store.

Ray Yonker nearly fell over when he staggered inside his shop and said that he only wanted a six-pack of beer. The liquor man joked that he surely hoped his most loyal customer wasn't buying from another seller. He assured Yonker that he wasn't cheating, and he even purchased a pint of Ten High to prove his allegiance. He also promised he'd be back by tomorrow once he'd finished his hunting business in the woods.

On the drive back to Joe's farm, his hands started shaking on the wheel again. His crystal eyes were seeing haints all over on the road. "They ain't really there," he mumbled, attempting to coax himself to sanity. "They ain't there. They ain't there."

By the time he turned off Highway 21 and onto the gravel

road to the farm, his bladder was about to burst. He stopped the Ram and hopped out for a piss. While he stood with his urine streaming into a bubbling puddle, the trees around him began to close in. Their movements spooked him so bad that he halted his piss in midstream and rushed back to the Ram with his pants undone.

The November sun was slowly descending into its coffin as he drove down the high hill slope toward the cabin. He glimpsed the horses and jack bucking across the pasture, and it occurred to him that he had not fed them today. He drove on to the barn and loaded bales of hay into the truckbed. He then went out to the field to meet the hungry herd. While cutting the bale strings with a rusty Barrow knife and spreading the hay out upon the cold ground, he reached and petted their wet noses, and whispered how gallant they were, and how he wished he could be one of their kind.

Full darkness had devoured the sky by the time he stepped into the cabin. He renewed the dead fire. Hoping the light would hold off the hallucinations. He warmed a can of beef soup on the stove. Then while wolfing his meal with two remaining beers, his mind began to worry about haints again. So he opened the pint and tilted it back for short swallows.

He wandered off to the bedroom. He came out hauling his hunting clothes and boots in his arms. Though they stank of his sweat and the wildness of the woods, he gracefully laid them onto the calfskin chair like a virgin bride on her wedding night. He picked up the clock from the mantle. Set it for a time to ring. He shed his green flannel shirt and his tan colored trousers. He then reclined himself onto the couch and pulled the scratchy Mexican blanket up to his chest. And there he rested, as the firelight flickered shadows about the darkness.

A minute passed. Five more. No haints appeared. Nor the spectacle of his faceless boy. He shut his eyes and trusted the fire would keep the terrors of the night from sneaking into his drifting slumber.

30

THE HEADLIGHTS OF FIREBIRD BEAMED low as it snaked through the tornado-wrecked streets of Newtown and arrived at the rundown Cullen house.

Pen parked in the street and got out and took the grain sack of clothes from the backseat and lugged it to the front door. It was still slightly ajar from yesterday's visit, so he nudged it wider and tossed the grain sack inside. Then he trekked back to the car to get his duffle bag. He also thought to grab the week-old beef jerky stored inside the console since there would be no supper tonight.

Once he settled inside the only home he had ever known, he plopped onto the pea green couch and allowed his eyes to adjust to the darkness. The room was as cold and grim as a cave. He slumped back onto the torn cushions and rubbed his arms to warm, and his mind again began to gauge the cruel ironies that had formed his wayward life. How he had been the repo man for the bank that was now repoing his family's worth. How he had come into the world as the unwanted son of a hateful father. How he had unknowingly fathered a dead son he would never love.

Round and round his troubled thoughts spiraled on the quirks of his fate, until he concluded that maybe something outside of himself had been governing his choices all along.

God, maybe. Or lack of one.

He lifted himself off the couch and grabbed his duffle. He pulled out the pen and the tablet. He opened it to find the rendition of Tara that he'd drawn a couple of nights ago. He ripped it out and crumbled it and tossed it into the corner with the rest of the discarded trash.

He flipped the tablet to a black page and began to run the ink across the paper with the preciseness of a ballet dancer on stage. The vernacular exteriors were drawn first. The parking lot and entrance and exit onto Central Avenue came second. Next were the guts of the place. He scribbled in the lobby and teller windows and offices, trying to be precise with the right dimensions and lengths. He then moved onto out-of-sight locations that he'd not seen since he was the janitor. The drive-up window in the back. The hallway where check-counting machines sat. The safe with its rounded vault door that dated back to the 1960's and weighed 38,000 pounds. His memory recalled how Mr. Hobson had once showed him where the security cameras were concealed, and how the lenses filmed in grainy black-and-white with no sound. He also remembered the banker had once showed him a dye-pack hidden inside a stack of fake twenty-dollar bills, and for fun they had tested it by exploding the red ink inside an empty currency bag.

He stopped to study his art. He envisioned himself running around inside the sketched lobby.

He picked up the pen again and sketched a stick man

with a stick pistol pointed at stick customers and stick tellers and a stick bank manager, and as he drew them, he brought to mind the crime wisdom and robbery tales told to him by the old-school Russians. Grand and convoluted truths and fibs about how they'd pulled off masterful plans of thievery during their wild and youthful days.

OPENING DAY

31

AT MIDNIGHT THE CLOCK ON THE MANTLE RANG.

Byron's eyelids sprang open.

He yanked the scratchy Mexican blanket from his body and pulled himself off the couch to turn off the ringing.

Then with no self-inquiry as to the reasons for his sober state, he stumbled toward the bathroom down the hall.

After taking a lengthy stream into the stained stool, he shifted over to the sink and fixed his sight upon his likeness in the mirror. His interest then turned to the canister of camo make-up lying where he'd left it on the toilet tank.

He took the canister in his hands and twisted off the top and dipped his fingers into the colored gunk. Bringing a glob of it to his cheekbone, he began smearing it on like a Comanche brave grooming for battle.

After he'd coated his whole face into a green-and-black death mask, he wandered out of the bathroom, down the hallway, back into the living room, and beside the dim glow of the fireplace he gathered up the strewn articles of his killing vestment.

He first put on his tan trousers and green flannel shirt. Then he wiggled his bulky body into the camo coveralls that harmonized with his painted face. He plopped down onto the calf-skin chair to better squirm his feet into wool socks and camo boots, and then he crowned a camo toboggan onto his bushy head and crammed camo gloves onto his pudgy hands.

Rising up from the chair, his sight caught the half-empty pint of Ten High resting on the mantle. A potent impulse to have a quick snort shot through his bones. He stretched a hand and took hold of the bottle, weighing how little relief it housed. Though tempted for a burning bite, he shoved it into his hind pocket for later purpose.

He checked the clock. Twenty-past midnight. Six hours before dawn. His mind clear and oddly sane. He eyed the thirty-ought leaning against the wall. He slow-stepped over toward it, reached and gripped it by its walnut stock and slung it over his shoulder by its strap. Then toting it like it was some malformed appendage, he headed out of the living room, past the unlit kitchen, through the front door, and out into the chilly darkness.

The route took an hour of driving on the series of blacktop county roads before reaching the log road turn-off to Osage Bend. He steered the rusted Ram down the rutted path for another short piece until it ended at his parking spot.

The ride had been tranquil and warm from the heater vents blowing. But the moment he cut the engine a cold silence overtook the cab. And suddenly without the distraction of the long drive, his mind began beckoning the whiskey.

Not yet, he coaxed himself. *Not yet.*

He scrambled to find his water flask hiding under the seat and he chugged his thirst away. Then wasting no time for second thoughts or second plans, he stepped out of the Ram and slung the thirty-ought over his shoulder and ambled into the night woods.

Led by his instinct and the pale light shining from the three-quarter moon, he traveled over the humped hills and backbone ridges that he could read as well as the bones in his hands. The temperature was flirting with frost, but still he felt that this dark November morning was unlike the ones of recent. There were no clouds. No rain. No shrouding fog. He twice heard the hoot of a barred owl before it took wing. Later came the high-pitch yap of a coyote from the depths of a hollow. It was then he uncapped the Ten High pint, raising it in honor of his fellow night predators, and beckoning their kindred spirits to grant him good luck toward taking down his prey today.

He arrived at the deer-blind a little after three. Still more than two hours before dawn. For a short while he stood beside the black oak. Not moving. Not making a sound. Listening. His crystal eyes probing the moonlit darkness.

Then he walked on.

He scaled the side of a nearby hill and halfway up he arrived at a white oak whose wood was full in years. He placed the thirty-ought against its trunk, and with the heel of his boot he began to scrape the leaves and broken twigs away from its base. Once he was content with the three-foot circle to sit within, he planted himself down to the dirt and rested his back and head against the tree.

Minutes passed.

Not long now.

He studied the three-quarter moon and the not-so-bright

stars hanging in the black heaven. His fingers were beginning to ache from the cold wind, so he took out the pint to warm his bones and blood. Again, he sipped only a nip. He would not allow more. He would not wobble his rifle when the moment of truth arrived.

Be patient, he told himself. *Be patient.*

He set the pint down by his side and closed his eyes. He was afraid to see. More than his worry of a wobbly aim, he was dreading that the haints might appear and ruin his killing day.

It was after the trial judge had ruled that Sam Groat would be allowed to walk freely upon the earth that he became intent on sending Sam Groat to hell.

At first, he was just going to barge into Groat's house in the middle of the night and blow the sack of shit's head off. But he got the sense some folks might pity the child-killer as a victim that way. He wanted Sam Groat to die guilty of his sin. Die under mysterious circumstances. Die with questions that would never be answered. Die like the unfathomable death of his ten-year-old boy.

The eventual design of the killing came to him when he was still the deputy game warden. The job had required him to be knowledgeable of the areas where locals regularly hunted and the places where poachers illegally harvested their game. He also had to know the names and addresses of every hunter who bagged a deer or a turkey each hunting season. And whatever knowledge his memory could not store, the county record books could easily disclose. And so it was one night in his office when he opened the county books and saw that Sam Groat had killed five bucks in Osage Bend for five straight hunting seasons.

Over the past nine months, he had been scouting Osage Bend. Three to four times a week. Preparing himself. Stepping quietly and concealed among the trees. Becoming as perceptive to the sights and sounds and smells as the animals that call it home.

It was three weeks back, when the dying leaves were beginning to fall, he spotted Sam Groat trotting along a deer trail. A block of salt in his hands. He watched Groat lay the licking bait inside the worn-out tire. Watched him amble to the deer-blind that Groat had built himself by hand five years ago. Watched Groat ascend the short board ladder. Watched him hop on the creaking boards for a high view.

And it was at the moment that he foresaw himself shooting the sack of shit dead on opening day.

32

THE FAINT HUE OF TWILIGHT was spreading over the hills and the day critters were escaping their night holes and nests. A couple of chipmunks bickered on a granite stone while a gray squirrel scurried for acorns. A tufted titmouse chirped from a low branch of a hickory while a red-cockaded woodpecker tapped its beak high above.

Byron was still there, among them. Squatted in the dirt circle at the base of the white oak. His head leaned against its trunk. Asleep.

The crack from a rifle echoed from afar.

A puff of air huffed from his throat and he scrambled to recover from his slumber. Suddenly recalling where he was and why he was here, he gently twisted his head around the white oak and peeked down the ridge that lay behind.

Two hundred yards away was the rickety deer-blind. Perched in it was Sam Groat. He was wearing a blaze orange coat that stood out as sharp as a bullseye and a lever-action .30-30 Marlin rested on his lap.

A second gunshot clapped from the distant hills.

Byron's heart jumped a charge and he swiftly huddled behind the white oak. He discerned the sounds of guns as the telling report that the first bucks of the season were dead.

He collected his breath. Then he hastily removed the glove from his trigger hand. He found his fingers shaky from the low allotment of whiskey he had afforded himself, and he instinctively grasped for the Ten High on the ground.

The bottle lay on its side. Cap loose and spilled dry.

He closed his eyes and squeezed his fingers taut into a fist to hold off the shakes.

Then he reached for the Winchester.

He gripped the stock and swung the barrel around the tree trunk and pushed his right eye snug to the scope.

Though he could make out the human shape stammering on its feet for warmth, he could not hold the bouncing cross-hairs on the orange-capped head.

A crashing clatter then came running down from atop the ridge behind him.

The monster buck.

In its mindless yearning to rut with its stable of horny does, it wasn't carrying a lick of a watchful sense to the noisy racket it was making.

Groat could also hear the scuffling coming down the ridge and his bare face turned in Byron's direction.

Byron's pulse accelerated. Without thinking, he whirled up from his dirt circle and jerked the scope to his cheek.

The thirty-ought roared.

The bullet sailed a foot high over Groat's head and went far beyond into the woods.

Before Groat could figure out what had happened, Byron had pulled the bolt-action to chamber another round.

The thirty-ought roared again.

The second bullet ripped into a board of the deer-blind and Groat ducked down as if a hammer had pounded him.

"Don't shoot! Don't shoot!"

Groat's lips quivered as he waved the air.

He could hear the monster buck racing away through the leaves.

"I'm up here! In the tree!"

Then as Groat gingerly erected to take a closer study of the woods, the third roar came from the thirty-ought.

The winning bullet tore into Groat's gut. He tumbled over the side of the deer-blind and his body hit the ground with a sickening thud.

He buckled. Groaned. The hole in his belly seeping blood.

Within the next few minutes, the child-killer would die under mysterious circumstances.

Just as Byron had planned.

33.

AT TWENTY PAST NINE, a deer hunter was striding down a cracked sidewalk in a pair of scuffed Nikes. He was costumed in a buttoned orange hunting coat, orange ski mask, a pair of puffy camo pants, black leather gloves, and dark aviator shades.

When he came to Central Avenue, he stopped at the edge of the sidewalk and tucked his chin down as a blue Chevy Nova passed. Then he rambled across the street toward the Town & County Bank.

A few empty cars and trucks sat in the parking lot. No one else was loitering about. He kept his steady pace while he removed the aviator shades from his eyes and yanked the orange ski mask over his face. Upon reaching the glass double-door entrance, he sucked in a deep breath, withdrew a Colt .45 from underneath the orange hunting coat, and stepped inside.

His eyes scanned the lobby. Five customers in the teller lines. Three women. Two men. All older than fifty. Tammy Dixon and two other women tellers.

He rushed up to the largest man customer and smashed the poor bastard on the nose with the butt of the Colt. The large man howled and threw his hands over his face as blood milked from his nostrils and shoe-laced down to the checkered marble floor.

"No one fucking move!" the robber yelled out, dropping the timber of his natural voice.

Everyone craned their heads in shocked bewilderment as the orange masked man wagged a gun from frightened face to frightened face. From behind the two holes in the mask, his eyeballs rolled toward the chunky secretary named Susie sitting at her desk.

"Get the manager out here!"

Susie's eyeballs bulged as if to pop.

"Now fat girl! Move your ass!"

Susie shakily stood from her swivel chair and moved like a stunned sow toward the manager's office. Meanwhile, the large bloody-nosed man kept howling, so the robber kicked him in his rear to move him closer to other customers, waving the Colt like a conductor's baton.

"You, you, you, you. . . cram together! Come on, cram in!"

The petrified customers clumsily huddled together with quacking knees and eyes wet with fright. The robber then turned his aim toward Tammy and the two tellers standing stone still behind the window counter.

"How many others are back there?"

"P-P-Please don't h-hurt nobody," one teller moaned.

"How many?!"

"J-J-Just Kathy," the other teller stuttered. "Sh-she's workin' the drive-up window."

Then Ted Burns ambled out of his office, his face white as a bedsheet, his sweaty hands held high.

"Get over here!" the robber reacted, the Colt pointed sharply at Burns and the chunky secretary.

The sissy banker and his chunky secretary obeyed like dumb mules, stumbling forward.

"Okay, Mr. Manager, listen careful. You go over there and lock them doors, real quick, and if you try to pull any funny shit, I'll blow a hole right through you. You get me?"

"Y-yes," Burns whimpered, bobbing his bald head.

"And if you're thinkin' I might miss, you might also think about how you'll be stamped as the coward banker who ran away from all these poor folks for the rest of your life. Now tell me you understand."

"I, understand."

"Then go do it."

As Burns staggered toward the glass double-door, the robber yanked out a wadded-up grain sack from the inside of his hunting coat and tossed it toward the teller windows at Tammy.

"Take that sack and get whoever's back there at that drive-up window and fill it up with cash from the safe."

"I, I, I don't want no trouble," Tammy squeaked, her neck muscles clamping around her throat.

"The only trouble is if you don't do what I say, grandma, now get the fuck back there and do it!"

Tammy's eyes rolled back into her head, and she grabbed at her chest right before she tumbled to the floor. Then the drive-up window teller, a young blonde gal, stepped out from the door that led to the back room and vault. "What's all this racket--?

"Don't move!!" the robber roared, leveling the Colt her way.

She did as he said and froze.

The robber grasped that this was not how the old-school Russians drew up the robbery plan. None mentioned a heart attack. None said a teller would be jerking on the black-and-white marble floor like a choking trout out of the creek.

"Get up grandma! Get up!"

"She's got a heart condition," one of the tellers explained.

"Shut up!"

The robber's mind whirled with indecision.

"Window girl. Step over there to grandma and pick up that grain sack!"

The drive-up window teller shuffled toward Tammy and leaned down to pick up the grain sack. When she rose back up, tears were rolling down her flushed cheeks.

The robber's attention turned back to Burns, still standing in a fright at the glass double-door.

"Mr. Manager, get your ass back over here."

"Y-yes, sir."

Burns stumbled away from the doors, his eyes wide, not a single blink. The robber jammed the barrel of the pistol to his forehead.

"Give me those keys and get back there and help her fill that sack up with large bills. You do anything stupid like trip an alarm or put a dye pack in that sack you are going fucking die. You understand?"

Butt Burns bobbed his sweating bald head. Then the scared banker ambled abstractly across the lobby and stopped at a batwing door that gated the entrance to the vault room in back.

"I, I can't get in. I-It's locked."

The masked robber's darting eyes shot toward the drive-up window teller holding the grain sack. "Window girl, go let Mr. Manager in that fucking door."

Like a dutiful dog, the drive-up window teller swallowed her fear and hurried along to open the gate door.

"Make it fast!" the robber reminded them as they both rushed to the vault.

Now it was on to the next phase. Something the old-school Russians called *The Waltz*. The robber glared at all the horrified customers, his Colt at the ready in his fist.

"Alright, everybody. Find a dance partner."

The two men and three women customers and the chunky secretary shifted bewildered looks at one another.

"I said find a dance partner!"

The big nose-bleeding man turned to an old blue-haired woman, and the cross-eyed man trundled over to the elderly lady with a wart on her cheek. But the skinny third woman and the chunky secretary stood still in dread that they were going to be shot since they couldn't find a man.

"Partner the fuck up," the robber directed the women. He then gestured the Colt at the two tellers behind the counter.

"You too, do it!"

The two tellers linked up into a lovely pair, then so did the skinny woman and the chucky secretary.

"Alright, now I want all of you to kiss each other on the mouth and grab each other's asses like you've been waiting to make sweet love together your whole lives."

Again, the aloof participants hesitated over the outrageous demands. It all seemed like an appalling joke, and they were waiting for the masked robber to maybe shoot a plastic flower out of his pistol.

"I said grab an ass, goddamnit!"

"I'm a married woman," objected the wart cheek woman.

"You'll be a dead bitch if you don't mind me!"

With that, the lobby began to take on the appearance of a

dancehall in hell, as shaky hands seized upon clenched butts, and chosen pairs puckered up and placed their lips together. The two chubby tellers smacked like genuine lesbians, as did the chunky secretary and the skinny woman customer. The married wart cheek woman smooched a stranger for the first time in twenty-seven years, while the blue-haired woman's mouth became smeared with the blood of the big nose-bleeder.

"Now keep holding on to that ass like it's your own," the robber warned them, "cause if your partner tries to run, then you're both going to die."

Just as it seemed that *The Waltz* was calming the situation, Tammy went into cardiac arrest on the floor.

Then a shaking sound came from the glass double-door.

The robber twirled around and a tingle of alarm shot down his spine when he saw a goateed man curiously squinting through the glass from outside.

"Hurry it up, Mr. Manager!!" the robber yelled.

Goatee was shaking the locked double-door, wondering what in the world was going on inside the bank this Saturday morning. "You open today?" he hollered and knocked. "You open?" He could only see a gathering of folks who looked like they were cuddled and kissing, and there was a deer hunter standing amongst them.

The robber began to fret that the prying bastard wasn't going to shoo, so he yelled for the waltzing customers not to move, then he hastily hoofed it to the entrance.

He used Burns' key to unlock the doors and swung one open hard enough to thump the curious bastard in the face. Then he stepped out and poked the Colt under the man's hairy chin.

"Shut the fuck up or I'll blow your goddamn head off!"

He vigorously jostled the startled man inside and shoved him onto the floor.

"Wha-What's goin' on?"

"Stay down and don't move!"

The robber relocked the double-door. He then hoisted the new arrival back up and marshaled him across the lobby.

At the same time, Butt Burns and the drive-up window teller returned from the vault with the grain sack.

"You got all of it?!" the robber asked.

Burns and the drive-up window teller were too staggered by the profane hedonism in the lobby to speak.

"Hey! You get all the money?!"

Burns jerked back to his wits.

"Yes."

"Bring it to me!"

"Yes sir." The scared banker quickly trotted to the masked man pointing a gun at him.

"Window girl! Come closer so I can see you!"

The drive-up window teller hurried along as told, her eyes still wet from fright, and she halted beside the kissing blue-haired woman and nose-bleeding man.

The robber glared at Burns.

"Open it."

Burns' knees knocked together as he bent down and nervously pulled at the top of the grain sack. When the flaps opened, the robber stared in awe at the heap of wrapped bills bearing famous American faces. He estimated it to be a decent size inheritance from his dead rotten daddy and long-gone mom, plus about two hundred thousand in interest.

"You didn't put a dye-pack in there like I said not to?"

Burns gulped, giving himself away. "No sir."

The robber elevated the Colt at the drive-up window teller.

"Did he put something in there? Did he?!"

She was too traumatized to reply.

"Here, here, here," Burns spoke up, reaching into the sack.

He pulled out the wrapped bundle of 50s housing the dye-pack and held it up high.

The robber's hateful eyes glared murder.

"You stupid mother fucker!"

His gloved hand chambered a round and he shoved the Colt to Burns' temple, daring himself to waste the cowardly son of bitch who sent him that damn letter and had brought him back to this godforsaken town.

He raised and brought the pistol butt down onto Burns' bald head, and the banker slumped over, half-mindless.

The women screamed. The men hollered. Goatee broke toward the glass double-door. The robber spun and lifted the Colt and triggered.

The bullet exploded into Goatee's right calf and sent him sliding across the marble floor.

The robber's ears were left ringing as he scooped up the grain sack and torpedoed toward the double-door, unlocked it, and bolted out of the bank.

He came out running so blindly that he didn't notice the Buick Skylark pulling into the lot, and the car nearly clipped him, and the miffed woman driver laid on the horn until he lifted his pistol at the windshield and scared her, and then he went sprinting on Central Avenue, the grain sack bouncing across his back, and he kept running and running and running.

34

PEN ROCKETED DOWN CENTRAL AVENUE. The Colt gripped in his shooting hand and the grain sack bouncing on his back. The traffic was light this morning, and with only three blocks to the dead-end street of Euclid Way, he believed he might make it.

Then the bank alarm sounded.

It came much sooner than he had expected and was enough of a startle that his legs stretched their strides.

He cornered a short-cut onto Sycamore Lane. A few houses down he ran upon three youngsters tossing a football in the street. He diverted through a front lawn and recklessly raced through the maze of neighboring yards--leaping over fences and ducking under clotheslines and raising a chorus of barks from pet dogs. His thighs and hamstrings were burning and his shoulder muscles were constricting on his bones. Then when he shuffled out onto Grant Street his right leg gave-out altogether.

Down he went.

"Fuck" he growled.

He hopped back to his feet, heaving the heavy money sack onto his other shoulder, and he ran on with a gimp.

At the end of Grant Street, he hobbled onto Euclid Way and headed to the slumped vacant house at the dead-end.

He limped past the rusted mailbox, stepping on a crumpled newspaper in the driveway, then he angled around the house.

He shot through the backyard and stooped under a grove of shady bushes. Twenty yards back in the dark shadows of the trees he came to the spot where he'd left his duffle bag.

He dropped the sack of money and the Colt onto the ground. He began to shed his hunting get-up and Nikes. As soon as the orange had fallen from his body, he bent over to the duffle and picked out his anaconda boots and a gray sweater, and he began tossing on a different look.

Then out of nowhere came the stray bitch collie. Her nose sniffing along his trail. He took her to be a bad sign.

"Get!" he hissed.

The bitch cut away. But then she stopped and turned back with her one brown eye and her one blue eye gazing at him in demure judgment. He very much wanted to blow a bloody hole in her fucking head, but he feared the bang from the Colt would ring curious ears.

He went back to his changing, battling to ignore her, while the bitch never once sat or barked or even shook her tail.

After he'd fit himself into the general appearance of any common man not hunting today, he flung the deer hunting duds and his running shoes into the duffle bag. He hoisted it and the money-filled grain sack onto his shoulders and glared wrath into the hell bitch's two-color eyes.

"Go on, you damn dog."

Then he loped into the scrubland of thick brush growing wild behind the slumped vacant house.

The two acres of briar and bramble afforded him excellent cover, but the tangled thorns and spiky growth kept tugging to take away the bag and sack. They were also ripping gashes on his face and hands, and after a hundred steps of entering the prickly gauntlet, he looked as though he slept on a bed of broken glass.

He had greatly underestimated the amount of time and vigor it would take to bulldoze through the thicket, so as soon as he made it to the other side of the two acres, he tumbled to its edge for a breather.

He wiped sweat from his cut-up brow and looked past the nearby ditch to see the Firebird parked seventy-yards away on Birch Street where he'd left it. There were only four shitty trailer houses between him and freedom. No one was outside. No passing cars. Still, he knew that this was when and where he was most vulnerable to being nailed. So far, he matched the same description of thousands of other armed men roaming the woodland regions of Doe Run this morning, but any damn idiot with one good eye could tell Johnny Law about seeing a suspicious man with a stuffed grain sack and a duffle bag stumble out of the town thicket and get into a shiny black Firebird.

Time ticked fast.

His heart was rapid thumps.

He looked behind to make sure the hell bitch wasn't hounding his heels.

Then half-assured that it was somewhat safe to run on, he hopped up and went for it.

He didn't go at an all-out sprint, but his gimpy strides were lengthy and quick. He kept his unmasked face low.

Kept his darting eyes up. Kept his riveted mind on each of his steps to think of something other than the screaming alarm in his ears.

Once he got to the Firebird, he set down the grain sack and duffle bag and dug for the keys from his jeans pocket. He fetched them quick and popped open the trunk and pitched his baggage inside. He gently shut the lid to soften the catch and quick-stepped to the driver side of the car.

He opened the door and slid himself into the bucket seat, and when the door closed again, the distant scream of the bank alarm dimmed into the silent emptiness of the interior.

"Come on baby."

He inserted the key into the ignition, turned it, and his faithful black beauty purred upon first fire. He shoved the Colt snuggly under his seat and pulled the shifter into drive. His boot let off the brake and tapped the gas pedal, and the Firebird crept forward and rolled into the lane.

After he'd driven three slow blocks, he felt his lungs swell and release, swell and release--but then they seized the air inside his chest when his eyes peeped into the rear-view.

He saw a callous and cruel face bleeding scratches.

A face so severe, so malevolent, he couldn't say for certain if it was his or the face of his dead rotten daddy, and he kept staring at it until his fist violently swung up and knocked it off the windshield.

<h1 style="text-align:center">35</h1>

MOST OF THE ILL-MANNERED REGULARS who ate the Queenway Diner were out hunting in the woods this morning, and so, a more affable crowd of women and gentle townsmen were there sharing a peaceful Saturday breakfast.

Tara came shuffling out from the kitchen, carrying a water pitcher and mournful disposition. She had only to come to work today in hopes of driving away her compulsive thoughts of Pen Cullen, however her aim of forgetting about him had not yet succeeded. A piece of her was feeling a strange comfort that he now knew the truth. But the larger part of her was regretting that he had left Doe Run hating her again.

She moved upon a table of four sociable ladies to refill their water glasses, and one of them harped, "Did you find out what that alarm is all about?"

"They're just testin' the tornado sirens," Tara replied dully. "It goes off every other week. All you gotta do is look outside and see that the sky's clear."

"Thank you, hon," uttered a second lady. "Half a glass is fine."

A silence then swooned over the entire dining room when a camouflaged hunter staggered inside. His grease-smeared face carried the mask of death and his spooky gray eyes were blinking rapidly.

"Reckon that boy got tuckered out of the woods," a husband whispered to his wife. "Ain't even ten o'clock yet."

The hunter stumbled away from the door toward a window table and slanted down into a chair.

Tara finished serving the four ladies and turned back to the table behind her. "Would you like some water--?"

Her words stuck upon seeing the green and black hairy face staring down at the table.

"Byron?" she gasped mortified.

His crystal gray eyes tilted up at her.

"What are you doin' here?"

"You said anybody can be forgiven for anything they done. Ain't that what you said?"

Embarrassed, she glanced at the other customers in the room and noticed all of them staring back at her.

"You know you're not supposed to come here."

"I done it cause it was the right thing to do."

"You can't just come in here like this, I'm workin.'"

Byron rolled his eyes over the dining room, petrified that someone was judging him. To him the room was full of listening. He heard, not hearing. He saw, not looking. He gulped hard and ran his hands over his painted face, trying to lock down the lethal chaos stirring inside his head.

"How do they know?"

"Who?"

Tara had witnessed dozens of his loony antics during their

marriage, and many times she had put up with his crazy talk. But something inside of her soul understood this banter that he was now speaking of was far beyond the typical.

"What's wrong with you?"

"He got what was comin' to him."

"Byron, stop this. What do you want?"

"He got what was comin' to him."

His spooky gray eyes held fast upon her.

"Byron!" She clenched her jaws and darted a look at the spying customers. "You're talkin' crazy."

"I shot him. I shot him."

Her immediate thought was Pen.

Her mouth dropped.

"What did you do?"

"He's in the woods."

His wits were falling into a paralyzing psychosis.

"He's in the woods. He got what was comin'."

Tara felt the cold touch of death fall upon her shoulder. First her son. Now the son's blood father. And as she remained transfixed by the thought of death's new visit, neither she nor Byron noticed the black Firebird pull into the parking lot right outside the diner windows.

"In the woods," Byron repeated.

His glassy eyes wallowed at the four lady customers ogling him and he saw them as four grinning haints.

"Get away from me!"

He leaped up out of his seat.

"Leave me alone! Leave me alone!"

Tara ducked out of his way while the four ladies bound up and split from their table. Other customers clamped their teeth on their breakfast bites and a few more dropped their forks and knives on their plates.

"Get away from me!!"

"Byron! Stop it!!" Tara demanded. "Stop it!!"

He made a fast break for the door and Tara carelessly chased after him, her mind spinning over his cryptic confession.

"Byron! Byron!"

They both raced outside and found Pen Cullen standing there beside the black Firebird. His bare face was marked with red scrapes of dried blood and it gave the expression of cold murder.

Time ceased. It was as though the three of them had frozen inside their collective memories of days long dead. And just as it had been the last time they had gathered together, thirteen years ago at Byron's trailer, they spoke not with words, but with dubious stares upon one another.

"I shot him."

Pen looked at Byron, funny-like. Not understanding. Then his sight shifted down to the car seat where the Colt was lying at the ready.

Byron confusedly turned around at Tara, as if asking for her help, and he saw a horde of haints staring at him from behind the diner windows.

"Leave me alone! Leave me alone!"

He ran to the rusted Ram in a hollering fit as everyone else stood aghast and watched the insane hunter jump inside the cab of the truck and fire the engine and drive off in a squall.

Tara's pale face lolled toward Pen, searching for some sort of explanation or even a banal comment to the madness.

"Come with me."

She gave him a confused squint.

"What?"

"Come with me."

"Where?"

"Just get in the car."

She glanced back to see the nosy customers watching them through the diner window.

"I'm askin' you."

She recognized something doomed and hopeless within his voice. A desperate and lonely sound that drowned out the screaming alarm.

"Just come with me."

Then she recognized it.

It was the voice of God.

36

BYRON WAS DYING FOR A SHOT OF LIQUOR. But he didn't dare go to Yonker's liquor store for a celebratory bottle of Ten High like he'd promised because there was a haint riding shotgun in the Ram and it was clutching the Winchester in its claws.

"Don't you want a drink?" he heard the haint ask him. But he refused to answer back. He knew that if he replied it would mean that he was as insane as his insane mother had been.

"Boy you sure shot that fucker deader than dead. Course, it took you a few times, didn't it? What in hell happened to you out there anyway, lose your stomach for it or something?"

Byron looked over to see the haint sniffing the lingering tinge of gunpowder on the thirty-ought's bolt-action.

"Yes sir, you did it. And ain't nobody gonna find out it was you. Looks like nothin' more than a wild shot by somebody. Could be any hunter out there. Accident that could happen any day to anyone. But hell, even if they did find out, you'd be a hero. Wouldn't you? Wouldn't you be a hero, Byron?"

The haint laughed and laughed.

It stayed like this between them. All the way until noontime. The haint spouting betwixt comments and queries. Tickled by its own amusement. And it was still pestering Byron when the Ram began inching down the high hill slope overlooking the farm.

"You gonna eat a bite first? You should, you know. Never go on an empty belly, I always say."

Byron stayed silent and pulled up to the cabin and parked the truck and hurried to get out.

"What about the Winchester?"

Byron turned and stared at the evil thing. Then he gripped the thirty-ought and got out and slammed the truck door and headed toward the cabin door.

"Hey, where you going? You don't have time to go inside yet. You got to get busy burying things. Remember?"

Byron stopped and glared at the haint hanging its head out the passenger window. He knew that it was right, but he still refused to acknowledge it existed.

With the Winchester in hand, Byron trotted around to the side of the cabin. He came to a chopping block sat next to a rick of firewood and he reached and gripped the long-handle ax wedged into it.

"Don't hack off a toe." The haint chuckled. "Wouldn't be able to count to ten no more."

Byron placed the Winchester down onto the chopping block. He raised the ax over his head. The sharp steel blade came down and cut into the rifle, again and again. And with the fifth blow the butt end split off from the breech.

"Damn. I knew you were strong as a bull ox," the haint said, winking at him. "I'll have to put in a good word for you when you get there. Maybe they'll have a special job for you."

Byron paid no attention to the haint's promises and

continued to hack away at the Winchester's stock. Then once the thirty-ought had broken into a pile of metal and wooden pieces, he gathered it all up into his trembling hands.

He staggered toward a shovel leaning against the cabin wall. He reached and snatched it into his hand, then he lumbered away with the haint nipping at his heels.

They headed across the pasture. Byron in blank-minded oblivion.

They arrived at the bullet-riddled horse skull, still hanging twisted and loose on the sycamore. Byron dropped the dismantled rifle from his overstrained arms. Then with mad intent, he began stabbing the shovel into the ground.

Besides Missouri red dirt, the spade broke into rock and tangled tree roots. After ten arduous minutes of forking through the hard earth, sweat beads were dropping from Byron's grease-painted brow.

Still, he kept at it. Enlarging the hole. The haint hovering over him like a steely boss. Then when the pit had grown into a suitable size to bury his murderous secret, Byron's muddy hands let go of the shovel, and he went to his knees to scoop in the broken gun.

"Pretty smart hiding place. I always knew you was a clever one. A little heavy on the drinkin', but still a clever one."

Fighting to stay focused on the dirty work at hand, Byron began covering the hole with the mound of soil and rock he'd just dug. When he finished the burial and tapped down the dirt, he stood and leaned on the shovel handle to rest from his labors.

"Nice work. I'm sure nobody'll ever find it here. Maybe in a hundred years or so. But you'll be dead by then. Hell, you'll be dead today."

The haint laughed and flashed its sharp teeth.

Byron blankly stared into the haint's slanted red eyes.

"Why won't you let me be?"

"Let you be? Why, who would you have then?"

Byron brought up the shovel, threatening to swing.

"I said let me be!"

The haint's grin fell into a demonic snarl and its red slanted eyes widened into a full blackness.

"Who do you think you are, Byron Tisdale?"

Byron swung the shovel.

"Leave me alone! Leave me alone!"

Byron felt the haint's forked tongue slither inside his brain and the piercing pain caused him to scream.

"There is no alone! I am you!"

Then he gazed up to witness the haint burst into a bright red flame and vanish into thin air.

The pain was gone. He remained standing there alone beside the horse skull. He saw his mother. And Tara. He saw Joe Silva. His father. All of them stuck alive together. Like tadpoles at the top of a frozen pond.

He clutched the shovel and began walking back across the barren pasture. Halfway across, the jack and the gelding, along with the mares and the ponies, came neighing and fell in a line behind him, with the paint mare rushing forward to lead the horse parade.

When they all reached the weathered barn, Byron entered and climbed up into the loft. There, he began cutting bales with the Barrow knife and pitching the loose straw out the loft window, and as the bundles rained down into the corral below, the eager horses leaned their long necks and stretched their noses to nibble on the grand feast.

He climbed back down into the gut of the barn and roamed through the stalls, inhaling the stench of the ancient boards and the dead drifting dust and the shit of mice and swallows. He found a cracked-leather saddle without its stirrups, and he picked up a broken rein strewn across its horn.

Too short, he knew.

He wandered into the next stall. His crystal eyes searched over the rusted hand saws, the pickaxes without handles, and the dozens of other rusted relic tools scattered along the weathered walls, until his sight caught upon the rope coiled around a railroad spike.

He walked over to it. He took it in his hands. He realized it was too withered and weak. He pitched it to the ground. Spit. Then stumbled out of the stalls.

When he ambled into the main thoroughfare of the barn, he saw a spool of steel barbwire sitting inside a rusted red barrow. His rambling mind ran on different thoughts, trying to ride on just one. Then he looked up at the ceiling beam which ran from one side of the barn to the other.

That'll do, he knew.

He hobbled over to the barrow and took up the pair of cutters laying on top of the barbwire spool. He untied one end of the wire and walked backward to uncoil twenty feet. Then walked forward to double it together. The sharp barbs jabbed into his shaky and bloody fingers while he cut off the length. He then hoisted the spool out of the barrow and drove it under the beam.

It's time, he knew.

He lifted his feet and legs into the barrow one at a time and balanced himself upward. His breaths were coming and going quicker. He tossed the wire over the beam and tied it on tight with a hitch knot. Then with the other end he fashioned a noose.

He slowly slid the loop of spiked barbs over his crown

and dragged it down his forehead and face until he felt the steely points stick sharp into his neck. His hands lowered to his sides and his eyes peered through the open barn door to capture a last sight of earthly light.

He leapt.

And he was left swinging from the beam, as though he was some sacrificial effigy exalting eternal praise to some god from the forgotten past.

37

THEY HAD GONE FOUR HUNDRED MILES and out of Missouri. During the ride he had spoken little to her, and she little to him. The cause for the cuts on his face and hands he had blamed on a drunken ruckus with Byron, and she had no reason not to believe him after the bizarre scene she'd witnessed at the Queenway.

He hadn't mentioned the grain sack of cash in the trunk. Neither had he given their destination. North is all he'd said. North.

He'd been imagining Alaska. Ditch the Firebird outside Canada. Bus over the border. Buy a dependable truck or car from some shady seller. Then drive and drive until they reach the last frontier.

Around nine, they checked into a roadside motel at Tecumseh, Nebraska. He headed straight for a hot shower to soak his beaten and worn body which was besmeared with blue bruises and pink scabs. As the pulsating water massaged his aches, his haunted mind kept replaying what he had done today. Pictures telling the tale with different outcomes. Some showed Burns' brains splattered on the marble. Others showed the sissy banker with a lump on his noggin and dulled in a daze. Some had Tammy gagging no more breath. Others had her alive in a rocking chair. One showed the goateed man dead from a bullet hole in the back. Another had him limping on the sidewalks with a stick. Yet whatever made-up versions of his various crimes he'd committed, none of them could confirm or deny if he killed someone today.

When he shut off the water, he heard Tara's muffled voice from the room. Panic hit him. He quickly hopped out of the shower and cracked the door for a look-see.

She was wrapped in one of his clean button-up shirts and was sitting on the edge of the bed with the phone to her ear.

"I just feel that this is what I'm supposed to be doin'." She looked up and saw him staring at her from the bathroom.

"Who's that?" he asked, his scratched face showing concern.

"The pastor," she mouthed back. "Mr. Fox."

He wrapped a towel around his waist while his ears stayed tuned to her conversation.

"I know. I know. No, I'm not sure how long it's gonna be. But it's like you said, God is with me wherever I go."

He strolled into the room and picked up a pack of Camels from the nightstand. He lit one, listening to her with great interest, and sat down beside her on the bed. Tara could feel his edginess in her peripheral, and so she set to break off with the preacher.

"Okay. Well, I better go now. Okay. I promise to call back tomorrow. Yes, I'm sure. I'm sure. Okay. I will. Okay, I promise. Yes, I love you both too. Okay. Okay. I'll talk to you soon. Bye."

She hung up the phone.

"Everything all right?"

"I thought I should call and tell them I'm okay."

"You tell them where you were?"

"I told them just outside Lincoln."

"With me?"

"Yeah. They've been worried sick with not hearin' from me."

"That all you told them?"

"I said I's goin' away with you for a while."

"For a while?"

"Isn't that what you want?"

"What do you want?"

Her smiling pout showed her confusion.

"I'm here. Doesn't that tell you?"

He let a long stream of smoke go from his nostrils.

"What is it?"

Then he gazed back into her waiting eyes.

"We never go back there. Not ever."

Tara heard and understood the severity in his words.

"Okay."

"Not ever."

He placed his Camel into the ashtray. Then he reached and gently squeezed her arm to pull her down onto the bed pillows.

She laid her head next to his and snuggled close to his neck. And for a long while they lay like that together. Arm in arm. Staring at the sparkles on the ceiling.

Dreaming the same dream of all the tomorrows and tomorrows they would spend with one another.

ACKNOWLEDGMENTS

A huge thanks to Ron Earl Phillips. If not for your dedication to publish this novel with Shotgun Honey, this story might still be hidden away on a computer file or stuck inside a closet collecting dust.

Eric Roth, thanks for our longtime friendship and for reading all of my ramblings throughout the years, including our early times in the film business. It was always you who pushed my stories and scripts and project ideas onto the agents and producers who "make things happen," and without your support, I might've jetted out of LA decades ago and left this writing dream behind.

An echoing thanks to Husayn Frazier, the first person back in my college days in Florida who believed I had something as a storyteller. Without your friendship and initial spark to flame my own fire, I would have never ventured on this 30-year writing journey.

Rhett Frazier, the Okie. Thanks for partnering with me on those wild road trips to Mexico, amigo. I'm certain that many of our inebriated conversations unconsciously wound up as dialogue in this story. I'm guessing that someday our many buddy adventures will end up in another tale of some form.

My sincere gratitude for all of you who have read my work and offered encouragement, including the small indie publishers that have printed a few of my tall tales: Starlite Pulp Review; Cowboy Jamboree; 34 Orchard; Across The Margin; Pulp Modern; Punk Noir; Flyover Country; A Thin Slice of Anxiety; Dead Fern Press. Plus, a huge thanks to the killer authors who've praised this book — Peter Farris, Eli Cranor, Brian Panowich, C.W. Blackwell, Scott Blackburn, Meagan Lucas, Scott Von Doviak — and the whole community of fellow authors, scriptwriters, wordsmiths, and poets who keep tabs on me and each other.

And mostly, I'd like to thank my wife, Nuri, and our two daughters, Maya and Bella, for allowing me the time to escape into my creations, for if not, this novel would never have come to be.

SEAN JACQUES was born and raised in southern Missouri, and presently resides in Los Angeles with his wife, two daughters, and a bird dog named Rye. He is a literature teacher and author after previously working in the film industry as a screenwriter and script analyst. His short stories, plays, and poems can be found in several noir and grit-lit publications. *Doe Run* is his debut novel. See more about him and his works at seanjacquesauthor.com.

ABOUT
SHOTGUN HONEY BOOKS

Thank you for reading ***Doe Run*** by Sean Jacques.

Shotgun Honey began as a crime genre flash fiction web-zine in 2011 created as a venue for new and established writers to experiment in the confines of a mere 700 words. More than a decade later, Shotgun Honey still challenges writers with that storytelling task, but also provides opportunities to expand beyond through our book imprint and has since published anthologies, collections, novellas and novels by new and emerging authors.

We hope you have enjoyed this book. That you will share your experience, review and rate this title positively on your favorite book review sites and with your social media family and friends.

Visit ShotgunHoneyBooks.com

SHOTGUN HONEY
FICTION WITH A KICK
shotgunhoneybooks.com

www.ingramcontent.com/pod-product-compliance
Lightning Source LLC
Chambersburg PA
CBHW011807200726